THE DARK TOWER SERIES
General Editor: Gerald Early

This series features ꞏꞏꞏꞏꞏꞏ ction and nonfiction by African-American writers that reflect the varied and dynamic nature of the African-American experience.

BLUESCHILD BABY
by George Cain

A DROP OF PATIENCE
by William Melvin Kelley

THE FIRST BOOK OF JAZZ
by Langston Hughes

I NEVER HAD IT MADE
by Jackie Robinson

THE LIVES AND LOVES OF MR. JIVEASS NIGGER
by Cecil Brown

SPEECH AND POWER, VOLUMES 1 AND 2
Edited by Gerald Early

TRAGIC MAGIC
by Wesley Brown

Books by William Melvin Kelley

A DIFFERENT DRUMMER
DANCERS ON THE SHORE
A DROP OF PATIENCE
dem
DUNFORDS TRAVELS EVERYWHERES

A DROP OF PATIENCE

A Drop of Patience

WILLIAM MELVIN KELLEY

THE ECCO PRESS

THE ECCO PRESS
100 West Broad Street
Hopewell, New Jersey 08525

Published simultaneously in Canada by
Penguin Books Canada Ltd., Ontario

Printed in the United States of America

Published by arrangement with Doubleday, a division of Bantam
Doubleday Dell Publishing Group, Inc.

All of the characters in this book are fictitious, and any resemblance
to actual persons, living or dead, is purely coincidental.

Library of Congress Catalog Card Number 65-10609

Kelley, William Melvin.
A drop of patience / by William Melvin Kelley
ISBN 0-88001-460-1

9 8 7 6 5 4 3 2 1

FIRST ECCO EDITION

To Karen, my wife, with love.

INTRODUCTION

"It is quite possible," wrote Ralph Ellison in his introduction to *Shadow and Act*, "that much potential fiction by Negro Americans fails precisely at this point: through the writers' refusal (often through provincialism or lack of courage or opportunism) to achieve a vision of life and a resourcefulness of craft commensurate with the complexity of their actual situation. Too often they fear to leave the uneasy sanctuary of race to take their chances in the world of art."

How true this may have been for black writers in 1964, when this passage was written, is open to debate. Surely, at the end of World War II a generation of black writers, led by the monumental example of Ellison's *Invisible Man* and the fiction and essays of James Baldwin, tried to redefine black writing, distancing themselves from what they saw as the overtly social protest, Marxist-influenced fiction of Richard Wright, the most highly regarded black writer in America at the time. Led by Baldwin, Ellison, Gwendolyn Brooks, William Demby, and William Gardner Smith, the 1950s gave us black writers who were willing and able to enter the arena of art. Some, like Ellison, Brooks, and Baldwin, received great recognition for it. Naturally, it may seem that Ellison's allegation begs several questions: Are race and art mutually exclusive? Is there no such thing as a great racial art? Is race, indeed, a sanctuary or is it a province to which black writers, and black artists generally, are consigned by white critics who, in the end, determine whether something is art? These questions have preoccupied many black writers and to some considerable degree they are questions posed by William Melvin Kelley in his 1965 novel, *A Drop of Patience*.

The 1950s was the era of the Cold War, a time when many liberal intellectuals repudiated any overt or inescapable connection between politics and literature, repudiating the radical 1930s and the ideal of a proletarian art or the idea that the validity of a writer's art is as much a product of his political vision as his aesthetic sensibility. This thinking had considerable influence on many black writers. One has only to read Baldwin's essay on Wright titled "Many Thousands Gone" in *Notes of a Native Son* or read Ellison's account of the Communist Party in *Invisible Man* to know that many black writers of the 1950s were no longer interested in the possibilities of transformational or leftist politics as the doorway to a usable and liberating artistic tradition. Indeed, in this age of pressurized conformity, leftist politics itself, no longer held the seductive promise of liberation but rather seemed a prison of formulaic, restrictive, and predictable conventions. Baldwin, for instance, wrote that the impact of the seriously considered black protest novel that grew out of the failed proletarian struggle of the 1930s, "led us all to believe that in Negro life there exists no tradition, no field of manners, no possibility of ritual or intercourse, such as may, for example, sustain the Jew even after he has left his father's house." If this sounds a bit Henry Jamesian, a writer who exerted significant influence over Baldwin in the early stages of his career, it seems fitting in an era when the leading literary critic, Lionel Trilling, in his famous book *The Liberal Imagination*, came to James's defense over the popular naturalist writer, Theodore Dreiser, the darling of leftist literary critics in the 1930s. (Indeed, Trilling's dismantling of Dreiser's literary reputation is very similar to Baldwin's reappraisal of Wright and was undertaken for some of the same reasons.)

Baldwin's concern was shared by many black writers. In the 1950s black writers indeed tried to give us a fuller picture of African-American life and culture, a more complex set of black characters who were not necessarily driven or defined by race or by the condition of their oppression or whose tragedy was not a self-conscious discomfort with their race. It is important, though, to understand that this was no mere reactionary impulse. This movement of the 1950s was not an attempt to return to an earlier age before Wright's emergence. There was little interest in writing Victorian moralist fiction or the local color protest or accommodationist art of the turn of the century or the self-consciously racial art of the Harlem Renaissance, in which the predominant question was whether blacks should be depicted as primitives or anguished sophisticates. Nor was there much interest in the sort of folkish, dialect-driven novel of black cultural life that was the staple of Zora Neale Hurston. All of this was old-fashioned.

Whatever fault this new generation of black writers

found with Wright, it could not be denied that Wright was clearly a modernist writer of prodigious talent with a truly philosophical as well as sociological turn of mind and one who possessed a profound understanding of the dilemma of modern man in a mass society. Indeed, Wright's understanding of that dilemma made him an important influence for this post-war generation as the vanguard black existentialist writer. Doubtless, existentialism, theories of mass society and modern man, and the spread of psychoanalysis, which had an enormous influence on post-war white writers and critics, also influenced black writers and was clearly reflected in their work.

The other major influence of this new breed of black writers was jazz. By the 1950s, jazz had evolved into a self-conscious art music, played for listening, not dancing, audiences by small groups, not big bands anymore, in small clubs and concert halls. It was far and away the most seriously regarded art produced by African-Americans, having its legion of connoisseurs, its factions of critics, its amateur historians, its fan publications, its defenders and its detractors. The African-American jazz musician was the most seriously regarded black artist in America and, with the exception of a small number of American film-makers and American writers, was the most seriously regarded of all American artists abroad as well. The evolution of jazz from a dance hall, low-dive music for the marginalized (gussied up with pretentious symphonic flourishes or ethnically faked with jungle growls and driving tom-toms for many bourgeois white devotees) to a mainstream American popular dance music in the 1930s to an intricately performed, musician's music after the war is a fascinating story of how Americans define and consume art and how race is used as an effective marker and signifier for an art. To be sure, a few black writers like Langston Hughes and Claude McKay, who were major names before the war and were influenced by jazz, prominently featured it in some of their work. But for black writers after the war, jazz was an enviable exemplar of usable tradition, of the successful melding of race and art, of the black artist who could be taken seriously as a craftsman and a visionary. This is not to imply that black writers produced a spate of jazz novels; they have actually written very few. Nor am I suggesting that all black writers were or are jazz fans. I mean only to suggest that the evolution of jazz as a powerful art form that was simultaneously African-American and American was something that black writers hoped would happen for African-American literature. Doubtless, Kelley was drawn to a jazz musician as a protagonist for *A Drop of Patience* because Ludlow Washington, his blind hero, who was craftsman and visionary, both Tiresias and Vulcan, could be a stand-in for black America but also a compelling archetype for any individual black artist, even for Kelley himself. The brilliant critic Stanley Couch considers *A Drop of Patience* to be one of the finest novels ever written about a jazz musician. Certainly, this novel would be grouped with works like James Baldwin's "Sonny's Blues" and Dorothy Baker's *Young Man With A Horn* as one of the classic literary depictions of the jazz artist.

A Drop of Patience was William Melvin Kelley's third book. His first novel, *A Different Drummer*, published in 1962, and most likely partially composed in writing classes he took with John Hawkes and Archibald MacLeish at Harvard—apparently the only kind of classes that interested him there—was generally well received. His second book, a collection of stories titled *Dancers on the Shore*, was published in 1964 to a more mixed critical reception. Nonetheless, when *A Drop of Patience* was published a year later, Kelley was considered a name to be reckoned with among young black novelists. And he certainly figured prominently in the group that included John A. Williams, Paule Marshall, Kristin Hunter, Ronald Fair, Margaret Walker, Louise Meriwether, Alice Childress, Julian Mayfield, and John O. Killens.

A Drop of Patience appeared at a time when black America and black literature were undergoing dramatic convulsions, as indeed the nation and the culture as a whole were. Nineteen sixty-five marked the emergence of the Black Power movement, the death of Malcolm X, King's triumph and tragedy at Selma, the Voting Rights Act, and the Watts riot. It was also the year of poet and dramatist LeRoi Jones's departure from Greenwich Village to Harlem and the beginning of the Black Arts Movement, a vehement repudiation of the direction of post-war "integrationist" black writing. (Ellison, Baldwin, and Lorraine Hansberry were bitterly and occasionally viciously criticized during this period.)

The Black Arts Movement was to dominate black writing for the next half-dozen years, producing a great deal of agitprop and a relatively small amount of first-rate work. It was a movement largely generated to re-engage the black writer as a committed, politically self-conscious artist who would be producing art for explicit political rather than aesthetic goals. It was also a movement that was preoccupied with the theory of black writing: what should it be, whom should it serve, and by what criteria should it be judged? The answers insistently pointed to absolute liberation from white critical and artistic standards and white audiences. Regardless of the quality of the work or the overall philosophical aims, however, the Black Arts Movement was largely preoccupied with performance art, specifically theater and performance-oriented poetry. Names like Nikki Giovanni, Ed Bullens, Larry Neal, Sonia Sanchez, Etheridge Knight, the Last Poets, and Don L. Lee were popular, but none were novelists. It was not a particularly good time for the African-American novel. Kelley's work appeared, therefore, on the cusp, the end of one era, the beginning of another and represented a distinctly different sensibility and mood than that emerging in black literary circles.

A Drop of Patience is the story of a blind, black jazz musician, Ludlow Washington, instrument unspecified except that it is a horn of some sort, perhaps a trumpet. His narrative follows the mythical arc of the history of jazz music and simultaneously the mythical arc of African-American history. Born in the Jim Crow south, he is left by his father at a white-operated institution for blind African-American children. It is there that Ludlow learns to play his instrument. At fifteen, he is released to (purchased by) Bud Rodney, a black bandleader, and taken to New Marsails where he plays in a small dive called Boone's Cafe. In his sexual awakening and maturation, he seduces his landlady's daughter, marries her largely for sex, becomes a father, then leaves her when he gets a job offer in New York. Eventually, he becomes a leading jazz musician and starts his own band. He then has an affair with a young white woman, Ragan, who leaves him to return to her own milieu after she discovers she is pregnant. As a result of this rejection, he suffers a nervous breakdown on stage and spends several years in and out of mental institutions. He then meets Harriet Lewis, a black college girl with whom he returns to emotional health. He is rediscovered by the jazz cognoscenti but instead of returning to New York he decides to go find a small black church. "A place like that would need a good musician," reads the last line of the novel.

There are several thematic features to note about this novel: Ludlow is literally placed into slavery when his father leaves him at the home for blind children. Another inmate *claims* Ludlow, but when Ludlow asks if his master has a master he is told: "Stupid Slave! Of course, I does. We all got masters. You got a master as long as you live." The opening replicates incompletely the drama of New World slavery, with Ludlow being abandoned, placed in slavery, by his own people. But the scene becomes a more existential statement about the absurdity of human hierarchy, because Ludlow's master is literally no better off than Ludlow—is just as blind, and is himself trapped in the same institution. Ludlow's journey from the south to the north replicates the Great Migration. His affair with Ragan, the upper middle-class white woman, mirrors an integrationist phase of black history. (There is a striking irony that Ludlow is blind, therefore Ragan's color cannot, in and of itself, be any point of attraction for him.) Earlier in the novel, Ludlow tells his landlady how he first learned about race from one of the boys at the Home who told him that black people's hair was woolly and their noses bigger than those of whites. But Ludlow discovers that one of the blind boys with him in the Home has straight hair and a small nose, yet is black. What the novel suggests is that race is an illusion that blinds people who *can* see. His decision to return to a black southern church at the novel's end signifies a return-to-roots phase of black history. But the return to one's black roots is not a return to Africa but rather a return to the aboriginal black institution in America, a return, indeed, to a small black gathering. For, in truth, black community for Ludlow becomes a succession of small black gatherings, the Home, Boone's Cafe, the men on the bandstand, family gatherings with his fellow musician, Hardie (the name an obvious pun on what Kelley considers an enduring, virtuous masculinity as Hardie is both Ludlow's truest friend and a loyal family man), all versions of the family and home life Ludlow never had.

The novel loosely suggests jazz history as well. Ludlow learns to play his instrument in a home not unlike the Colored Waifs' Home where Louis Armstrong learned to play the trumpet. New Marsails, where Ludlow plays at Boone's Cafe, stands in for New Orleans; here Ludlow seems to be playing some sort of blues, black southern style jazz. When he is hired by black singer Inez Cunningham and goes to New York, he seems to be playing more in the style of swing. And all the while he seeks Norman Spencer, who represents a Bebop sensibility but also a connection with roots: Spencer's origins are playing for the rent parties that he enjoyed. In other words, Spencer is the idealized artist, both modern and traditional, the idealized jazz musician, intricately theoretical yet fulfilled by playing for dancers. Ludlow becomes a success playing something like Bebop or modern jazz, acquiring a status on the order of Dizzy Gillespie. His nervous breakdown resembles the emotional collapses of

Charlie Parker and Bud Powell. It is, once again, a remarkable irony that Ludlow goes crazy on stage, after Ragan leaves him, by putting on blackface and making insulting racial jokes, suggesting minstrelsy. Jazz as an art form never attracted whites as a minstrel art. Whites saw jazz as an outsider's music, a music that challenged standard bourgeois values, not as a music through which they could denigrate or degrade blacks. White jazz musicians never wore black face and black jazz musicians of the caliber of Ludlow were artists, not entertainers in any sort of minstrel tradition. Ragan herself represents a variation of the white bitch type one might find in the demimonde of the jazz world. Ludlow's return to a black church represents jazz music's attempt to return to its black roots.

On one level, one might say this is a novel about self-authentication through one's cultural expression and through one's history. But it is also about the nature of the art form itself. Should jazz be a listening music? Was it not better, more enjoyable as a dance music? Is the return to the black church meant to place the music not only in a more black milieu but a more truly functional ambience as well, where the music serves a more profound purpose than merely to be listened to for its sheer virtuosity? *A Drop of Patience* is, and this is unique, a jazz novel that does not deal with the cliched pathologies of the black jazz musician. Ludlow is not a drug addict or alcoholic. He is not even overly obsessed with art: seeking the perfect note, or looking for the transcendent sound, or trying to write the perfect score. As Whitney Balliet observed about the novel, "[Kelley] refreshingly treats his hero's music not as a sentimental banner but simply a craft that occupies only a part of his life." In short, neither jazz nor the jazz musician is romanticized in this novel. In fact, the jazz world as a social milieu is not conjured up with any specific detail. Playing music is Ludlow's way to make a living, nothing more, nothing less. Moreover, Kelley's novel does not suggest that jazz is a racial music or an exclusively black music. Indeed, in keeping with the mood of integrationist black writers, Kelley does not see jazz as a politicized art form. In a conversation with Reno, a fellow black musician, Ludlow does not buy the idea of jazz as solely the black man's art:

> Ludlow snorted. "I met some white boys who doing good things." "They just copying us, that's all. We do all the creating. Like you." Ludlow winced. "Listen, you do the playing and forget all other stuff. When you up there trying to put something together, you ain't got time to think about all that mess!"

But not all of Reno's racial thinking is wrong-headed. Just before Ludlow's breakdown, when asked what white people want from blacks, Reno replies, "They want us to be what they think we are." This touches the metaphorical heart of the novel—that blacks are forced to see themselves as others see them or to see themselves through other people's eyes. That is the true significance of the minstrel scene. It is also the true ironic significance of blindness in this novel, those who are forced to see themselves through the eyes of others are blind to themselves.

Gerald Early
St. Louis, Missouri
January 15, 1996

Had it pleased heaven
To try me with affliction; had they rain'd
All kinds of sores and shames on my bare head,
Steep'd me in poverty to the very lips,
Given to captivity me and my utmost hopes,
I should have found in some place of my soul
A drop of patience; but, alas, to make me
A fixed figure for the time of scorn
To point his slow unmoving finger at!

OTHELLO, IV, *ii*

PART ONE

INTERVIEW . . .

> *It didn't have nothing to do with art—not at all. What do a little kid, five years old, know about art? For that matter, what do I know about art now? I hear these critics talk about art and I say, "That's nice. But what do it have to do with me?" I can't figure it. I just play. That's how I earn my living.*

I

The house was too quiet. His little sister should have been running, screeching in the hallway; behind the house his brother should have been batting stones with a stick; his mother should have been singing. At least there should have been the short, heavy hiss of her broom. Instead the house was so still that the dripping of the kitchen pump was as loud as rocks dropping into a pond.

The house had never before been this quiet—and during the past few days it had been more noisy than ever before. His father had been carrying heavy things out of the house, returning with a lighter step, his load left somewhere behind him. Several times his mother had cried. Earlier this morning he had thought they had all been tiptoeing around him, whispering, then leaving the house and going away. He thought perhaps his mother had kissed him. But he was not certain. He could not always tell if he was awake or dreaming.

But he was sure he was awake now. He felt awake. He lay on

14

his back, his hands moving over the bare mattress, his fingers squeezing the small cotton balls his mother had told him held the bed together. Once he had crawled under the bed, into a dust-filled space, and gripped the cold springs in his hands. He could not understand how such soft cotton balls could hold the bed together.

Finally he sat up, swung his feet onto the splintered wooden floor and bent from the waist, searching for his coveralls. Finding them, the downside damp from the night, he pulled them on and stood up. Perhaps they were on the porch.

He felt his way quickly down the hall. The wall was chipped and scarred in several places, his favorite scar shaped like a hand missing one finger. Under the plaster was a frame of wood.

The tiny wire squares in the screen door were hot. Pushing against the door, he made the spring pop and whine. On the porch his face and his chest, bare except for the bib and straps of his coveralls, began very quickly to blaze. It was late in the morning; the heat was coming from high up. No one was breathing on the porch.

He stood in the heat for a long while, waiting for someone to come for him. He could not go with his friends (who seemed to be playing in the cool woods behind his house); he did not want to be away when his parents returned. Finally, feeling his way to the edge of the porch with his bare feet, he sat down, dangling his legs over the edge. Tall, tough grass grew near the porch and tickled his swinging feet.

Someone came when the heat was on top of his head. He had just put his hand to his hair and found the tiny curls and beads burning when, in the road running past the porch, pebbles began to spray. A man was walking fast. He recognized the footsteps, which stopped at the head of the path. "Papa?"

"Come on, Luddy. Come on, son." His father approached him, dragging his heavy shoes. Ludlow smelled dust in the air. Then his father's hand lifted his own and Ludlow hopped to his feet. His father led him to the road. They went to the right. The dirt on the road was so powdery and dry it felt like hot water. Ludlow complained and his father lifted him up, his arm under Ludlow's thighs like a seat. Ludlow put his arm around his father's neck. Whiskers pricked his fingertips. He wondered where he was being carried, whether or not his brother, sister, and mother would meet him there. The ground under his father's feet turned hard; Ludlow felt the shock all the way through his father's body. They were on pavement now. A car chugged by, blowing warm air against his face. They were on a highway, but it must be different from the one to which his brother had always led him; he and his father had turned the opposite way.

His father was marching now, his steps regular and heavy. Ludlow bounced on his arm. Small stones crunched beneath his father's feet. Cars came toward them, bubbling, and blew past.

They turned off the highway. Not far away, birds whistled and clattered in the trees. There was pavement again, and steps. His father leaned against a heavy door and carried him out of the heat. Ludlow's bare arms grew cold. Away, in a long, echoing space, children were talking.

His father put him down, but held his hand. The smooth stone floor sent a shiver through him. A chair skidded and squeaked, and footsteps went away, limping. A moment later, the limping footsteps returned, accompanied by another set.

Ludlow smelled cigar smoke. "This him?"

"Yes, Warden. This him. Luddy. Ludlow Washington, sir." His father squeezed his hand.

"Looks older'n five." The cigar smoke jammed into Ludlow's nose.

"He five, sir." His father was frightened, the first time ever. "Honest to God."

"Don't matter." He paused. "You can write your name, can't you?"

His father let go his hand. "Yes, sir."

"Well, then tell him to sit down. My assistant'll look after him. We got papers to sign." The Warden turned away. "Watch him." The cigar smoke faded with his father's footsteps. The Warden's assistant limped toward him, clutched his arm and snatched him forward. "Sit there and don't make no squawk." Ludlow was spun around and pushed back onto a wooden seat. Running his hands over it, he discovered it was a bench, with arms at either end.

"What you doing there?" The assistant was now some distance away. "I told you not to move!"

Ludlow sat rigid, his palms flat against the bench. After a few moments the assistant's chair scraped and the man's step disappeared behind the far-off sound of the children. Ludlow remained rooted. It could be a trick, the kind his brother sometimes played when he told Ludlow to wait for him because he was going away for a moment. Ludlow would follow his brother's steps away until he was certain his brother was gone. Then he would move and his brother would yell, close again, having sneaked back. They would laugh at his brother's trick. But Ludlow knew the Warden's assistant was not playing.

He sat quietly, trying to decide where he might be and why he and his father had come. Something in the air of the place stung the inside of his nose. Though it was summer outside, inside it was cool and damp. It must be a big place because of the echo that surrounded everyone's words. Far away, the children still talked.

He knew he had never been there before. He wanted to leave.

A bit frightened now, he attempted to make himself feel better by sucking his thumb and humming a song his mother had taught him.

"Who that humming?" The voice was hoarse and wet-sounding, like his brother trying to whisper through a mouthful of water. Before he could answer, two hands skittered over his face, the fingers poking in and out of his nose, eye sockets, and mouth, then around to his ears and the sides of his head. They brushed over his hair, then paused. "I don't know you." The watery voice was bewildered. "What you doing here?"

"I don't know." Ludlow too was bewildered. Never before had he met anyone who did the same thing he would have done had he encountered a strange object or person.

"You don't know? Well, I guess I do. You got any money?"

"No."

"What's your name?" The hands moved to his shoulders and down his sides.

"Ludlow Washington."

The hands were searching his pockets now. "How old?"

He hesitated. "Five."

"I'm six." The hands left him. "You'll be on my floor, the third. You remember voices good?" Ludlow nodded. "You remember mines because I'm claiming you for my slave. I'm your master."

"What?" He did not understand what the boy was talking about.

The boy's hand touched his nose, slid across his face, grasped and twisted his ear so it burned. "I said I'm your master."

"Master?" Tears tickled Ludlow's cheeks, but he tried not to make the sounds of crying.

"I'm your master. That mean I own you and when someone

ask you something, you tell them to ask me because I'm your master, and I do your answering. That's everybody excepting the Warden and Mister Gimpy. All the boys here."

Ludlow was certain he would soon be leaving, but he decided he would play along with the boy. "Do you—"

The boy slapped him across the face. "When you talking to me call me Master."

Ludlow sighed. "Master, you got a master too?"

The boy twisted his ear before he answered. "Stupid slave! Of course I does. We all got masters. You got a master as long as you live." His hand left Ludlow's ear. "I'll talk to you upstairs. Remember I'm your master."

"What you doing there?" The Warden's assistant yelled at them from a great echoing distance. When his shout faded, his limping footsteps were running toward them.

"Wasn't doing nothing, sir. Just making friends with the new boy." The boy was very polite now.

"Just get away from him."

"Yes, sir. I just leaving, sir. Good-bye, Ludlow. Nice to meet you." The boy's step was soft and quick.

"Didn't I tell you to sit still?" The assistant's voice was over him now. "After them papers is signed, I'll teach you to listen better." Not even his father had ever sounded as angry. He wondered what would happen after the papers were signed.

The assistant backed away. It was quiet now and Ludlow listened for the children. Their voices were shrill. He began to feel lonely. His stomach was upset. He wished his father would return soon and take him into the heat, outside to the call of birds, to the smell of hot tar and grass.

The Warden's voice was coming toward him. "Remember you give up your right to complain. You signed him over to us and

19

we'll teach him to earn his way. But this ain't no nursery; it's a school."

"I don't cause no trouble, sir. I'm just grateful you took him." His father was happier now.

Ludlow did not know whether or not to stand up. He remained in his place. The two men stood over him. His father's voice was higher up, farther away from his ears than the Warden's. "I'll tell him if you want me to."

"Surely, go on. It'll save us the trouble."

The bench sagged as his father sat beside him. "Luddy, I got to tell you something." There was a long silence. Ludlow reached out and found his father's arm; the man was sweating. "You ain't the same like most kids . . . you special . . . yeah, that's it, you special. And I got to leave you here to learn special things. . . ."

He did not really know what else his father said to him. He turned up toward his father's voice, realizing that the boy and the Warden's assistant had known all along. He was staying. He even knew he was staying for a long time. He did not know where he was or how far he had come, and could not get home alone. He began to cry.

Then his father was standing, his hand on Ludlow's head, making his brittle hair sizzle. "Good luck, Luddy." The hand was gone.

The Warden and his cigar were near again. "We can handle it now." The assistant's chair strained and in a few seconds, he had grabbed Ludlow's arms. Ludlow struggled to get free, but could not.

"You better get out now." The Warden was angry.

"Yes, sir." His father's voice came at him. "Good luck, Luddy." Heavy shoes echoed away, meeting the sigh of an opening, closing door. Ludlow started to kick his bare feet at the assistant and received a burning, ringing slap on his ear.

"Third floor," the Warden shouted.

Recovering from the slap, Ludlow began to scream for his father.

"And for Christ's sake, get him quiet!"

Ludlow was lifted into the air, still kicking and yelling. He was carried across the stone floor, above the clicking of the assistant's limping step, was put down, and, without warning, was slapped across the face more times than he could count. He stopped crying and began to moan. "Is that better now, you little bastard?"

The Warden's assistant grabbed him by the wrist and pulled him up three flights of wooden stairs. When they reached the final landing, Ludlow's hand was numb. A doorknob rattled and he was pushed over a doorsill into a room filled with children. The assistant was behind him, holding his neck tightly. "Hey!" The voices stopped. "This is Ludlow Washington." His voice went to the right. "You! Four-Eyes! You're to see his bed gets aired if he pisses in it. If it ain't aired, you sleep in it."

"Yes, sir." Ludlow did not recognize the voice.

The assistant let him go and slammed the door. Ludlow stood very still, waiting for the voices to start again. A great many scraping steps circled in on him, whispering. Then they began to paw him. Their hands moved over every part of him, especially his face and head.

"His ears is like bowls."

"He surely got a big head!"

"Must be a ugly little bastard."

"Wait a minute. Let me have a touch." All hands dropped away except one. "That's him. I found him first, downstairs. I told you." It was Ludlow's master. He was almost happy to recognize even his watery voice. "Ludlow Washington?"

"Yes."

"Yes, master." His master twisted his ear. He was about to cry, but decided not to bother. He realized it would do no good, and only nodded.

"Ludlow Washington, you my slave. The rest of you boys hear that? This my slave. Right, slave?" His master's breath was on his face. "Say it."

Ludlow shuddered. "I'm your slave."

Just so he would never forget, his master twisted Ludlow's ear one last time.

PART TWO

INTERVIEW . . .

It was just like this. I went in the Home. They said,
"You taking piano." Everybody took piano. Then when I
got to be nine, they said to all the nine-year-olds, "You
playing sax, and you playing trombone and you playing
trumpet—" and like that. I didn't have nothing to do with
choosing what instrument. That's what I was trying to
tell you before. But I did practice good, because I could
tell music was better than a tin cup on somebody's corner. And when I was sixteen I got out the Home and
went with Bud Rodney's band which was working at
Boone's Café in New Marsails.

I

Ludlow boarded at a house near Boone's Café. His room was seven paces long and five paces wide—more space than he had ever in his life had to himself. There was a bed, long, narrow, and hard, and a blistered dresser. There was even a window on the street. Most nights, when the air was heavy, people laughed and joked below the window and music from four or five neighborhood jukeboxes spilled into his room. From a stand at the corner, spicy barbeque sauce opened his nostrils. Both before and after work he would sit by his window, fingering his instrument. He had been out of the Home for three months.

For as long as he could remember, starting when the Warden told him his family could not be found, he had been counting the days to his eighteenth birthday when he would no longer be a ward of the state and could leave the Home. There was to be no formal ceremony—just his eighteenth birthday and a summons to the Warden's office. The Warden would tell him he could leave, and perhaps that a job had been arranged for him.

But Ludlow's call had come well before his eighteenth birth-day—a month after his sixteenth. The Warden had told him that as of that day, and for the next two years, he would be in the custody of a Mister Bud Rodney, a Negro bandleader in New Marsails. Ludlow was to pack his clothes at once. Rodney would arrive at the Home in two hours to pick him up.

Returning to the room that for the past eleven years he had shared with twenty boys, he tried to figure out, but could not, how all this had happened. He decided to ask Rodney as they rode into New Marsails.

"Might as well get it straight now." Rodney was a head shorter than Ludlow and his whining voice came from below Ludlow's ears. "You out the Home because I paid good cash money for you." He stopped, probably waiting for Ludlow to reply. But Ludlow was too surprised to say anything, though he could not help wondering how much he had been worth. Rodney went on: "I seed you play last year at the State Competition." There was a yearly contest of all the bands from state-run schools and homes. "I figured someone'd be offering you big money sooner or later, more than I could pay, but I wanted you in my band anyway. So I went to your Warden and paid him a little sum and he signed you over to me." He was quite proud of himself. "So now get this straight, little boy. You my son now and for two years you don't play for no one else and you don't cause no trouble. Because you do and it's back to the Home." Ludlow nodded. He had been sold, had a new master, but at least he was out of the Home. He relaxed and enjoyed the ride; he had never before been in a car.

It had not turned out badly. Mister Rodney paid him a better salary than he could have gotten anywhere else, though it did not take him long to discover he was getting only a third as much as anyone else in the band. None of it mattered. From time to time,

27

he wondered about his old master, who, slaveless now, would not leave the Home for still another year.

The house where he lived was owned by a middle-aged woman, Missus Bertha Scott, who clomped across her creaking wood floors as if her feet too were made of wood. She liked Ludlow at once; it was in her voice. Although she was not running an eat-in house, was just renting a room, she would sometimes feed him in her kitchen. Ludlow did not know if he liked her, for he had been around too few women to be able to decide. Sitting in her kitchen, eating her food as she knocked from stove to cupboard to icebox, he would let her do most of the talking. "I don't got nothing against musicians. Most folks thinks them is ungodly, but I reckon Jesus'd forgive musicians their vices just as soon as he'd forgive the Thief." This day she had fixed a special stew for him and now she was at the stove tapping a portion onto a plate while he sat, stroking his silverware.

"God must love music too—all kinds. I reckon you can't help the places you got to play it in, with them hussies in their tight dresses. And even some of them is good girls, just gone wrong. Here you is, boy." The dish rang as she set it down between his hands. He tilted his head, waiting for her to tell him the location of the food on the plate, but as usual, she forgot.

"Ma'am, you—" He spoke out into the room, not certain where she had gone.

"Beg pardon, son. Now let me see how you do this thing." Her breath warmed the left side of his face. "The stew's at from four o'clock to eight o'clock. I give you some peas and they about at nine and ten. Couple pieces of corn bread at twelve, and a boiled potato at one and two. Glass of water off the plate at twelve. You got that?"

"Yes, ma'am. Thank you." He picked up his fork, aimed it

28

where the stew would be, and felt it glide into a chunk of meat. He raised it to his mouth and chewed, juices coating his throat. He went for the potato, but it slid away from him, the fork hitting the plate.

Missus Scott had clomped around the table and seated herself across from him. "Oh, I shoulda mashed that a bit. Here." She pushed the table slightly and took the fork from him, rapping. "There now. How . . . how long you been afflicted, boy?"

"Ma'am?" His mouth was full.

"How long you been—"

"All my life, ma'am."

She clicked her tongue. "That's a shame. What's it like?" They had never before spoken of it.

He tried to answer, but could not. He had never been able to see and so knew only vaguely what he was missing. He sat silently, his fork moving slightly across his plate. "I don't know, ma'am."

She said nothing for a few moments, while he ate. He felt uncomfortable, knowing if he reached out and touched her face at that moment, he would find a frown.

"Don't you got no idea of what the world's like?"

He put down his fork. "Oh, yes, ma'am."

"Like what?"

Once again, her question sent his mind scurrying. "I know all about smells and sounds and shapes and all things like that. But there's some things I don't get. I asked the men in the band about some of them, but they just laughed."

"I won't laugh at you." No voice he could remember had ever sounded quite as gentle. And though many times before he had been ridiculed and even beaten for asking questions, he decided to risk asking once more. Still, he was shy and unsure. "Well, ma'am, it's about the difference between people."

"Are you asking me to tell you about men and women?" She was stunned and amused.

For an instant, his blood ran hot. He knew next to nothing about sex, but still he did not have this in mind. He had enough sense to realize he would have to find out such things from someone else. "No, ma'am, that ain't it. I mean, between colored folks and white folks. What about that?" He waited tensely for her reaction.

"Oh." She was frightened. "Well, I don't know. . . ."

He retreated. "That's all right, Missus Scott. . . ."

"Wait now, boy. I'll try, but I ain't smart. What you know already?"

He tried to recall the bits and pieces of knowledge he had scraped together. "There was a boy at the Home called Four-Eyes—he wore these really heavy glasses. He could see a little bit, you know. So anyway, we used to ask him. He said the Warden and Mister Gimpy was white. So we'd ask what he meant and he'd say there was two kinds of people, white and colored, who was mostly brown, and that we was all colored because all the blind white boys was in another place because the law wouldn't let them be together with us because they was better. So we asked why they was better and he said because they was white. So we was back where we started from." He took a breath. "Well, I did notice that Mister Gimpy and the Warden spoke different from us. So we asked Four-Eyes if it was being white made them talk different. And he'd say, Yes, kinda. Then he'd say white folks most always had straight hair and their noses wasn't as big. But there was a boy in the next bed and I'd felt him and he had straight hair and a tiny nose where you could feel the sharp bone in it. And we'd ask Four-Eyes if he was white and he'd say, No, he was colored too, but very light in color. So then we was back at the start again." When he finished he was out of breath and trembling, excited to have said all this.

Missus Scott sat across the table, breathing, but nothing more. Behind her, water boiled, and behind that a car, many blocks away, blew its horn in the afternoon street. Finally she cleared her throat. "I ain't smart, like I said, but it seems like all the things your friend told you was true, even if some was opposite to others. There's colored and white folks. I reckon you can tell that most of them is colored because they is kinda brown and because they most all got something like big lips or bad hair or flat noses."

"What about the white colored ones?"

"I reckon they colored because they say they is. And some of them say they ain't and fool everybody." She sounded bitter and added quickly, "I ain't condemning them like some do. It so hard being colored that, quiet as it kept, maybe I'd say I wasn't colored if God give me the chance. But I ain't exactly no snowball."

"It bad to be colored, Missus Scott?" He did not feel bad and wondered if he was just stupid.

"White folks say it is and I reckon most colored folks believe it."

"Why?"

"I reckon they been told it often enough to believe it."

"No. I didn't mean that. I mean why does white folks say it?"

She hesitated before answering. "Boy, I can't tell you nothing at all about how white folks think, just what they does!"

They fell silent and Ludlow tried to sort out all she had told him. At the end, he knew no more than he had known before. But he was grateful. She had tried. She was simply not smart enough to know any more than he did. He wanted to know one more thing. "Missus Scott?"

"Yes, Ludlow." Her voice was hoarse.

"Missus Scott, can I touch your face?"

She sighed; her chair scraped around the table and came bumping to rest next to him. "Go on, boy."

He rested his fingertips where the tired, hoarse voice had started. The lips were as thick as two fingers, soft and fleshy. Above, two huge holes breathed warm air. Not far above that, the bridge of the nose was flat, separating two bulging balls. The forehead was broad and greasy, and the hair was as coarse as broomstraws.

He had an idea of the answer to what he was going to ask her, and sensed he might hurt her, but he had never been able to ask it before and might never again. He knew he must. "Missus Scott, white folks think you ugly?" He kept his fingers near her mouth so he could feel the answer.

"Yes."

"Then I'm ugly too."

"Yes, you ugly too." She stopped, then chuckled, but her mouth was drawn tight. "Sometimes I think even the best-looking of us is ugly to white folks."

He nodded and took his hand away. He did not know what to do with it, and so found his fork and began to eat his stew.

2

Boone's Café was a long, barnlike building with a high roof that swallowed the band's music and much of the chatter of the drinkers. People came to Boone's to talk, sometimes to dance, but very seldom to listen to music.

Several prostitutes worked out of Boone's. They would stand at the bar, to the right of the bandstand as Ludlow played, drinking and waiting. Two of the girls, Malveen and Small-Change, had adopted Ludlow soon after he came to work. When he finished a set or a solo, they would shriek and applaud him; they would pat his head when Otis Hardie, the trombone player, led him from the bandstand.

"Here he is, ladies." Hardie waited until Ludlow put his hands on the smooth wooden bar before he let go his elbow.

"He so good tonight! He such a swinging little boy!" Malveen was the taller of the two, her high bubbly voice almost level with Ludlow's ears. She had hugged him a few times and he knew she was plump and soft, her breasts held loosely in her bra. He was

33

too shy to ask to stroke her face and did not know if she was as pretty as her voice made her seem. "When you paying me a visit, Ludlow? You don't need to bring no money, sweetness."

"You bitch! If he visiting anybody, he visiting me. You don't know how to treat no young boy. Young boys got to be taught. You'd smother the child." Small-Change was short, her voice dry. She always seemed angry.

"Lying on you got to be like lying on razor blades. Young boys don't want no bag of sharp bones. Ain't that right, Ludlow?"

Having had no experience, Ludlow did not answer. The two women bewildered and embarrassed him.

"See there?" Malveen mistook his silence for support. "He visiting me!"

"He didn't say nothing, you bitch." Small-Change swallowed and clicked down her glass. "Besides, we too old for him. He need a young, churchgoing girl. Not all bent and bruised like you— and me too." Her hand was on his cheek. "We be looking out for you, child. I got a sister upstate about your age. She go to church regular."

Hardie spoke from beyond Malveen. "I ain't too young for you, is I, Small-Change?"

Louder now, her answer traveled along the bar, in front of Ludlow. "For you it five dollars extra, for linen."

"Look, Small-Change, here come Mister Heavyballs. His girl wouldn't get up off it." The warmth went out of Malveen's voice; a potential client had wandered into the bar.

"Well, see you now, Ludlow," Malveen bubbled. "Take care of yourself."

"You brung a coat, didn't you, honey?" Small-Change patted his back. "Look like rain."

Both girls sighed and left. Hardie came to Ludlow's side, his glass scraping along the bar toward him. "They fun, ain't they."

"Yes." He had not taken his hands off the bar. "Say, Hardie, can I ask you something?"

Hardie gurgled, then answered. "Sure, go on."

"Well . . ." he hesitated, knowing Hardie would laugh at him. He decided to brave the laughter. "Well, Hardie, it about . . . you know . . . screwing?"

"What?" Hardie shouted, then howled. Ludlow felt sweat tickling his brow. "What you want to know about it?"

He felt sure many people had turned toward him, astonished at his stupidity. He wished he had some liquor in his fist, but his guardian, protecting his investment, had forbidden Ludlow to drink. He whispered toward Hardie's laughter. "I got raised in the Home and there wasn't no girls out there. All I know is talk. And that ain't nothing."

"Sure. I get you." Hardie's tone had changed. "I'll tell you everything, only Rodney's signaling us. I'll tell you on the way home." Hardie took his arm, pulled him gently away from the bar, and started him up the steps to the bandstand.

"You take the first two choruses, Hardie. Ludlow, you take three—and make them good, a little honking at the end." Rodney's voice whined above piano chords. "We got big folks here tonight and I don't want to be made a fool."

"Who, man?" Hardie placed Ludlow's hands on his instrument, which was atop the piano, then dropped his arm. Ludlow knew the stand perfectly if first he located the piano.

"Never you mind! Just big folks, is all." Rodney played several more chords. "Make it *Rent for Rodney*."

Altogether there were six men in the band. With the exceptions of Ludlow and Hardie, they were all at least forty years old. Hardie was twenty-two. He was a good trombone player; like

Ludlow, he should not have been in Bud Rodney's band of tired old men.

His back pressed against the piano, Ludlow listened to Hardie's solo and thought over all he already knew about women and making love to them. Most of his information had been gleaned from the bragging of other, older boys, some of whom had not lost their sight until their teens. "First thing, you grab a titty and hang on. Then you stick your hand up her dress and when she starts to breathe heavy and steady, man, you know she ready!" Ludlow was certain such advice was not at all reliable. He finally decided, somewhat ashamedly, he knew nothing about women. He would just have to hope Hardie could explain things to him. But Hardie could only instruct; he could not make love for him. Ludlow would have to find the girl himself—perhaps Malveen if she was not just fooling about his going to visit her. And besides, she would know so much and might laugh at his lack of knowledge. For an instant he was embarrassed in advance, but then angry with himself; he resolved he would not worry about being embarrassed. Every man had made love for the first time.

Hardie finished his solo. Ludlow stepped forward and began to play. He felt good now, having made a decision, as if he had grown years in the last few minutes. At the end of his solo, Hardie whispered in his ear. "Rodney say take two more." He did, the bass line steady under him. He tried to play so fast that his fingers ached. When he finished and lowered his instrument, there was some applause, a rarity in Boone's Café. He bowed and stepped back. They applauded through a good half of Rodney's solo.

Hardie came to his side. "Inez Cunningham's here. She's Rodney's big folks. She was clapping her ass off for you. I thought her eyes'd fall out."

"Inez Cunningham? No stuff?" He had listened to and liked all her records. She was the most important jazz singer in the country. "She like me?"

"You knocked her out." Hardie's voice smiled. Rodney finished off, followed by some of the others, then they played the closing chorus. They did seven more numbers and filed off the stage. Hardie led Ludlow to the bar, where Malveen waited alone.

"He wanted Small-Change. Guess he wanted to punish hisself." She was bitter. "How's my boy?" Ludlow did not answer and she continued. "I heard you playing just now. Oh," she groaned, "you get to me, little boy. You better stop playing like that or I'll forget myself."

Hardie snorted. "You can forget yourself with me any old time."

Ludlow's hands were flat on the bar, water, missed by the bartender's rag, under his fingers. "She really like what I was playing?" It had never really occurred to him before that anyone could be moved by his playing. Music had been only his way of staying off the corners with a tin cup in his hand.

"Of course I did, honey." Malveen put her arm around his waist.

"Not you, Malveen." He turned to Hardie. "I mean Inez Cunningham."

Hardie cleared his throat. "She was on her ass."

"Who you niggers talking about?" Malveen realized now she had missed something.

"Inez Cunningham's here. Sitting over there." Hardie's voice turned away.

Malveen's necklace rattled. "Oooh! Ain't she beautiful! Look at her hair. It look most naturally straight. And them clothes. Ludlow, baby, you should see them clothes she got on. I could work on my back fifty years and never get a dress like that over it."

Hardie laughed. "She sure look fine all right."

Ludlow only half listened to them. There must be some people who lived for music, to play it and hear it played. Perhaps Inez Cunningham was a person like that. There was no other reason for her to come to a bar filled with drunks and prostitutes.

Malveen must have been staring at the singer. "There's your boss, sucking up to her."

"Rodney bending over her table like it a God damn altar." None of them spoke for a moment. Then Rodney was talking to them.

"Inez Cunningham wants to meet you, Ludlow. She liked the way you played. Maybe she thinking about asking you to go with her. You can't go nowheres. You got that?"

"Yes, sir." For an instant Ludlow thought of his old master, could almost feel his ear being twisted.

"Come on then. Hardie, you bring him." Hardie tapped his elbow. Ludlow grabbed Hardie's elbow with his fingertips. They moved between tables, past laughing voices, through the smell of liquor and stale smoke.

"Here he is, Miss Cunningham, my star soloist."

Ludlow let go Hardie's elbow and extended his hand.

The hand which took his was small, soft and cold, with long fingernails. "Nice to meet you, Ludlow." The voice was the same one he listened to on the jukeboxes, perhaps a little higher. It was Negro and Southern, but not as much of these as his own or Malveen's. "Now sit down. Who's your friend, the trombone player?"

"Excuse me, Miss Cunningham." Rodney, eager to please, introduced Hardie.

"You're not bad either, Hardie, but Ludlow has you beat." Her voice smiled.

"I know that, Miss Cunningham."

Ludlow was surprised at the humility in Hardie's voice. He had not realized Hardie felt that way about his playing. He hoped he was not jealous.

"Go on back to your girl, Hardie. She looks lonely."

Hardie laughed. "Nice to meet you, Miss Cunningham. You keep telling them."

"I will."

"I'll come back after while, Ludlow." Hardie's footsteps disappeared into a tinkling glass and a woman's shrill laughter.

Ludlow was sitting now, his hands gripping the edge of the table. He knew that Rodney was at his right. Then there was someone else at the table who had not yet spoken.

"Well." Inez Cunningham moved closer to him. Her perfume was so cool and fresh it seemed to clear his nose. "Over here, on my right side, is the leader of my group, plays piano. Say something so he'll know you."

"How you doing, Ludlow?" Her pianist was old, and probably fat. His voice, not resonant, seemed to come from far inside him.

She sighed. "How long you been playing?"

"Seven years—what I'm playing now. Before that I played piano a few years. I mean, I started on piano."

"You come along fine in seven years. Who you like?"

Ludlow named a few famous musicians; all but one played his own instrument. The exception was Norman Spencer, who played a rugged, old-fashioned piano.

"Norman? He thinks he's still in a marching band." Inez Cunningham did not approve.

"He makes me laugh sometimes. I mean, he'll be going along

and then he'll crack a joke right through his fingers and he'll make me laugh. You know what I mean?" She probably would not. He had never met anyone else who liked Norman Spencer.

"I can't imagine that old bastard laughing at anything." She turned to her pianist. "Can you?"

"Not me. I ain't never even seen him smile."

Ludlow did not know what to do. He did not want to seem rude, but she had after all, asked him his favorites.

"Well, anyway, that isn't what I wanted to say to you. I want you to come with me."

His lungs seemed to stomp on his stomach. She had asked him. He had to turn her down. Rodney must be looking at him now.

Inez Cunningham went on: "I know Rodney doesn't want to lose you. But I don't care about him. I need you. What you say?"

Behind him a woman was quietly accusing her husband of cheating on her, a drunk was laughing, the cash register belled. He could not tell her the truth, that Rodney had a hold on him. That would ruin Rodney's reputation and his guardian would be angry. "I'd surely like to go with you, but I can't. I . . . promised Mister Rodney I'd stay with him until I was eighteen. He did a lot for me, got me out the Home, and I want to make it up to him."

Rodney answered smoothly. "Awh, Ludlow, you know I don't hold you to nothing. You can go when you want, especially when you got an offer like this one."

"See there, Ludlow? He's not holding you." Inez Cunningham was pleased with Rodney's generosity.

"No, Miss Cunningham, I made a promise to myself and I got to keep it."

"Shit!" She drew it out as if it were the last word of a ballad.

Ludlow knew he would have to get away from the table now. He had never before thought that music would take him any-where and now he realized it could quite possibly take him all over the world. He stood up. "I'm sorry I can't go with you."

In a moment, Hardie came to get him.

"When you decide you've paid your debts, you write me. Maybe I'll still have a job for you. I only hope you as loyal to me."

"I got to warm up now." He could not bring himself to say good-bye, simply grabbed Hardie's elbow and moved away from the table.

At the end of the evening, in the early morning, Ludlow, his cane hooked over his arm, followed Hardie toward Missus Scott's, guided by his own gentle grip on the trombone player's elbow. It had rained. From time to time, drops, shaken by a slight breeze, fell into small pools in the pavement. A car passed, its tires on the asphalt like a quickly opened zipper. The air smelled fresh, a bit salty from the Gulf of Mexico. Hardie told him what it would be like with a woman, instructed him. . . .

Inez Cunningham would be singing. Her voice would come up from the hissing rain-soaked streets and into Malveen's win-dow. Malveen would have told him that evening she had not been joking, that if he would, she would be honored if he de-cided to go home with her. They would walk to her place, the rain from the trees and rooftops dripping in the long, echoing alleyways. Her room would smell of the same perfume Inez Cunningham used. As soon as she closed the door and turned the key, she would begin to undress. He would stand waiting—miraculously unclothed, but not naked—waiting, listening to Inez Cunningham and Malveen's clothes falling to the floor.

Then Malveen would sigh for him, walk to him and put her arms around him, kiss him. Her breasts would flatten between them. She would lead him to her bed. He would lie beside her, would bury his head in her soft breasts, would kiss them, would take a nipple into his mouth and roll it on his tongue. She would moan and he would know she was ready for him. At that moment, he was sure, he would know exactly what to do.

3

Ludlow had just come downstairs to ask Missus Scott
to sew a button on his band jacket. He could have done it himself
had he a needle and thread; they had taught him at the Home.
As he felt his way down the narrow hall leading to the back of
the house and the kitchen, the sound of new footsteps met him.
They were younger and quicker than Missus Scott's, but had
the same heaviness. He stopped, registered them as those of a
big woman, then went on, his fingers finally catching the door-
jamb. He stood with his feet on the sill. The heat of the kitchen
enveloped his face like a washcloth. Missus Scott and her visitor
were cooking. "Missus Scott?"

"Hello, boy." She was happier than usual. "Come in. I want
you to meet somebody."

He inched just inside the door.

"Ludlow Washington, this is Etta-Sue, my daughter." There
was great pride in her voice.

Ludlow remained in place, waiting for a sound, a voice to

which to speak. The new footsteps stopped in front of him. "Pleased to meet you, Mister Washington." Her voice was high and tense; she was almost as tall as he was.

He extended his hand. Hers was too large, too coarse, too strong for her squeaky voice.

He nodded. "Me too."

"You come down for something special, Ludlow?" Missus Scott was standing across the room by the hissing gas, stirring in a pot with a wooden spoon.

"I won't trouble you now, Missus Scott. It just a button. Maybe you could let me hold a needle and some thread."

"Ain't no bother. I'm cooking, but Etta-Sue ain't doing nothing. You'll do it, won't you, honey?"

Etta-Sue said nothing and Ludlow remained motionless, deciding what to do. Finally he reasoned Missus Scott would not have offered for her if the girl did not want to do it. He extended the balled-up coat. Its weight left his hand. "Where you keep the sewing basket, Mama?"

Missus Scott was turned away. "In my room under the bed." There were two steps. "Come on in, Ludlow, and sit down." She was facing him now. "I made some lemonade."

Knowing the kitchen quite well by this time, he walked forward to the table, felt out a chair and sat down. Missus Scott was dropping chunks of ice into a glass, pouring the lemonade over them. She set the glass before him just as the quicker heavy steps returned and her daughter sat across from Ludlow, sighing.

He was uneasy about her doing it. "You really don't have to do that. They taught me how."

The wicker basket rasped open. "Ain't no bother, Mister Washington. Mama wants me to do it." She rattled through the basket, then closed it.

"I appreciate it." He sat back, uncertain.

Missus Scott knocked her spoon against the pot and set it down on the stove. "Etta-Sue's a maid in a white folks' mansion up in Willson City."

Willson City was the state capital. Ludlow had never been there, but now at least he had something to say to Etta-Sue. He had been squirming against the heat and silence of the room. "Must be bigger than New Marsails."

"Newer. Not bigger." The words were tight, as her lips must have been.

Since he had left the Home, Ludlow had met only girls like Malveen and Small-Change. Sitting now, the kitchen chair hard against his buttocks, the heat sticking his pants to his skin, he wondered if all respectable girls were as tight-lipped, distant and unfriendly as Etta-Sue. Or perhaps this was simply her attitude toward him, the attitude that people who worked in the daytime had toward people who worked at night. He wondered if perhaps his blindness had silenced her, made her unable to find something to say to him for fear of insulting or hurting him. Whatever it was, he did not like her. "I do appreciate you mending my jacket."

He had expected her to reply once again that it was no trouble, but instead her voice came up from her lap and asked him about his job.

"It a good job. I make good money."

"I bet you good too. I'll have to walk over and listen to you." He was surprised, and could not tell if she was serious or making fun of him.

Missus Scott had laughed. "You better not go into that joint. I'll snatch you bald-headed!" She was joking, but her voice had a hard edge.

45

The girl's voice turned toward the other woman. "I'll go in there if I want." She was slightly angry. "Maybe I just will come over." She spoke to him again. "I ain't taking orders all my life." She mumbled the last.

"You do that." He was not encouraging her to come.

Finally, over the gurgling of what was boiling on the stove—he thought greens—came the snap of broken thread. "It finished, Mister Washington." Her chair scraped back and her footsteps came around the table. "Here." The coat dropped into his lap.

He stood up and thanked her, assuming she was in front of him. "I got to practice now." With one hand on the edge of the table, he checked his position and started to the door. When he felt the room open up into a blast of cool air—the doorway—he stopped. "I guess I'll see you later. Thanks again."

"No bother." Missus Scott answered, at the sink now. He did not know where Etta-Sue was standing.

He went down the hall, found the figure of a plump cherub perched atop the glass-smooth but sticky knob at the foot of the banister, and climbed to his room. His instrument, out of its case, was lying on the already made bed. Every morning for eleven years he had made his bed, readied himself and his belongings for the Warden's inspection; now he could not break himself of the habit.

He picked up the instrument and, without putting it to his lips, ran up and down the scales. The notes popped and bubbled in his head. When he made a mistake in fingering, he would know that too. He could practice for hours silently, knowing exactly what he was playing. He sat down by the window. It was the middle of the afternoon; the sun's heat came directly into the window and he began to sweat. Below in the street a jukebox was playing Inez Cunningham's latest record. There seemed to be no musicians behind her, just her dark voice in the heat. Two men passed, talking loudly about how much they hated their jobs. Someone in the neighborhood was cooking ribs, someone else ham with cloves. There was perfume and the hammering of high heels, a woman laughing, then a man, then the woman again.

He began to think of something Hardie had told him: "You just got to stay calm. The first time it happened to me, I didn't stay calm. I was like a dog what couldn't wait to get out the house. And the girl knew. She told me she'd had real men and wasn't wasting no time with no little punk like me. So now when it come your way, stay calm, like you done it seventy-eleven times before. Even if she tells you her thing is on the bottom of her left foot, you stay calm. Because once they know they better than you, they'll wreck you."

Then he was thinking about Etta-Sue Scott:

He would be coming home, tired. His throat would be tight and sore from playing, his lips numb. He would turn the key, lean against the door, and step into the stillness of the house. Then he would know Etta-Sue was standing at the foot of the stairs. "Mister Washington?" She would scrape toward him in bedroom slippers and he would know she wore only a night-gown.

"That you, Missus Scott?" He would not let her off easy, would make her plead for him. She thought she was special; in the daytime she despised him because he worked at night in bars, because he was blind. But at night she would want him to make love to her.

"No. It's Etta-Sue. You know. Etta-Sue Scott?" She would be afraid he would send her away, that he might have nothing to do

47

with her. She would move close to him and try to put her arms around his neck, would try to kiss him.

He would hit her. To teach her an important lesson, he would reach out and find her face with his fist.

A step away now, she would gasp and cry, but softly because she would not want her mother to awaken and discover her downstairs with him. She would cry and attempt to wriggle into his arms, pleading with him to make love to her. He would be able to feel her nightgown, soft like the summer curtains in Missus Scott's living room.

He would hit her again, knocking her to the floor. She would be sobbing now and, following her sobs, he would find her, would grab the hem of the nightgown, pull it up around her waist, run his hand across her thighs, and finally, would slide into her. On either side of her head, he would grip the dusty carpet beneath them. Through her sobs, she would tell him that she loved him. . . .

In the street a fire engine went by, the bells clanging, the big tires rumbling. He stood up and put his instrument on the chair, and went to the bed. Taking his handkerchief from his pocket, he lay on his side, unbuttoned his fly, and thought about it all over again.

4

Just before the beginning of the last set, Ludlow found himself alone at one end of the bar with Malveen. It had been a slow night for her. Small-Change was now making her fifth trip, having described him to Ludlow as a one-time-a-year man. She had assured Ludlow and Malveen she would be back in fifteen minutes. "I don't think he'll even get one up."

Malveen had made only two trips. She had been standing at the bar now for nearly two hours, drinking steadily. At first, she had not seemed to care that she was having a bad night. "I made my rent, my food for this week. I can even buy a new dress if I want. Hell, I ain't about getting rich anyways."

Ludlow had noticed that Small-Change usually got more business and had asked Hardie about it on one of their walks to Missus Scott's. "It in her face, Ludlow. I mean, you got to think what kinda man is using whores. Malveen's prettier, I guess. But Small-Change look like she'll do anything. I mean, *anything*. She look crazy. You take one look at that face and you know when she takes you to her room and you pay your cash, something weird'll happen to you. And ain't that just what you looking for if you got to buy it?"

But what Hardie could see in her face, Ludlow could not find in Small-Change's dry, bitter voice. And though both women had hugged and fondled him, only Malveen set loose his imagination. He had been thinking of her more and more, always wondering if she was serious about wanting him to visit her. He wanted to believe she was, and finally he did. He decided the next time she invited him to her place, he would risk asking her if she meant it. He was glad that Small-Change and Hardie (who was somewhere in the café trying to secure his own invitation) were not there; if Malveen turned him down, laughing at him, at least no one else would be present to ridicule him.

The set before he had tried to play especially well; it was his music that usually started Malveen. But besides saying that he sounded good, she had said nothing. He waited, silent in the chatter around him, for her to speak.

Finally she sighed and he asked her what was wrong.

"I ain't losing my looks, is I?" She paused. "Hell! You can't tell me." She swallowed and banged her glass on the bar. "It just that I don't like the scorecard: five to two. It a matter of pride. Maybe I got to get a new dress—something that shows more." She was slurring her words; she was very nearly drunk.

Momentarily Ludlow forgot his own preoccupation. He did, after all, like her a lot and did not want her to be unhappy. "What you wearing now, Malveen?"

"It green, you know, smooth stuff. And it's low in front." She pulled in her voice, speaking more to herself. "Maybe it ain't low enough or something. And it got some beads on it. It's nice. Here, feel." She took his hand and placed it on her stomach. The cloth

50

was smooth. Under the material, he felt her stomach rising and falling. His thumb just grazed the bottom curve of her breasts. She let go his wrist and without really knowing it, he did not immediately remove his fingertips from her stomach. Finally, suddenly embarrassed, he pulled back his hand and held the bar tightly. He had a strange sick feeling and his ears were numb.

"I don't know how that skinny bitch do it. A man sees me across the room and comes over. I know he looking at me. But when he gets here, she sneers at him and I end up ordering another drink and she leading him out the door."

Ludlow thought about what Hardie had told him, but decided not to tell Malveen.

"You used to love me." Her voice smiled. "But I bet you don't even want me no more."

Hardie had told him to stay calm, but against the hardness of the bar, his hand began to shake. "Yes, I do." He had meant it to be low, relaxed, almost joking, but instead he sounded like a little boy trying to convince his friends he was courageous.

Malveen did not seem to notice. She spoke at the bar in front of her. "Sure, you do. You my steady boy friend."

"No, really, baby." He hated too the way this came out. He waited for her reaction. Now she would know what he had been thinking. He would find out if she was serious.

"Why, Ludlow." Her tone was indulgent. "You ain't making love to me, is you?"

"What you think, baby?" He tried to imitate how Hardie would have said it, and it sounded just like an imitation, not at all real or relaxed, rather false and shrill.

Malveen began to laugh.

Ludlow's forehead grew cold, then damp. "What other offers you had lately?" He had not realized how much he had wanted to hurt her for laughing at him. For an instant he wondered from where had come the impulse to hurt.

"I guess not many." She took another swallow. "Besides, you don't got to jump so salty. I was only laughing because I always figured you thought I was your mama or something."

"You ain't nobody's mama." It came out smoothly and surprised him. For an instant he was no longer nervous, frightened. Hardie had been right; when the time came Ludlow had known what to do, what to say.

The only close sound was Malveen's breathing. She was staring at him; he could almost feel it. "All right. I'll wait for you." She said nothing more. Ludlow stood beside her, his left foot on the metal rail running along the base of the bar, his right foot planted firmly but his knees slightly limp, his palms sweating. He was breathing heavily.

She had accepted. He realized that he had not expected her to accept. Not only that, but he began to wonder if he had even wanted her to accept. Perhaps it would have been enough for him simply to muster the courage to ask her. But she had believed his few smooth words, though as soon as they were alone, he was certain she would know exactly what he was, what he had done. Perhaps he should have told her the truth, that he had never made love to a woman, and then asked her to be kind enough to teach him. He could still do this—and she would laugh at him so loudly, would ridicule him so ruthlessly that he would choose to go back to the Home rather than meet the people at Boone's again. He stood beside her thinking all this, until finally Hardie came to rescue him, leading him to the safety of the bandstand.

He did not play very well. The few notes to which he paid any attention were shaky and uncertain. But Rodney said nothing to him; no one else must have noticed. While playing, he went over what it would be like, what he would do, rehearsing again an often thought dream. Finally, the set finished, Hardie, to whom he had told his plans, and who had warned him once again to stay calm no matter what happened, led him back to the bar.

"Here's your man. Treat him right." Hardie seemed to be teasing them. Ludlow wondered if he was jealous.

"You're a bastard." Malveen had continued to drink and sounded very like Small-Change. Ludlow thought about calling it all off, telling her he had been fooling, but it was too late for that now. He had to finish it. Besides, she would be different when they were alone.

Hardie told them to have a good time and left.

Ludlow waited at the bar, his cane hooked over his left arm, his instrument case in his right hand, his other hand clutching the smooth wood. "You—you ready, Malveen?"

She bumped against him; she was quite drunk. "Sure. I'm ready." She was defiant. "Let me finish my drink. You don't want me to lose the money I paid for it, do you?"

Ludlow put down his case on the bar, but kept his cane. "No."

She gulped her drink, put down the glass and grabbed his arm. "Come on, honey." For an instant he could smell only the alcohol on her breath. Then it was gone and he had picked up his case and she was half leaning on him, half leading him to the door. In the street she kissed him on the cheek. "That bitch! I bet she be jealous when she finds out you going home with me. We'll have a good time."

Ludlow clung to his case, wishing he had left it under the bar. Malveen's breasts rubbed against his elbow, the smooth, slick-sounding material, then a seam on her bra and under that her skin. He staggered under her staggering weight. They passed few people. He kept thinking, knowing it was a silly thought, that everyone they passed suspected why he was with her and was watching him.

"Oh." Malveen stopped short after five minutes. "This is it. We almost passed it. This is it." She led him up three wooden steps, onto a creaking porch, and stopped again. "I feel dizzy."

"You all right?"

"Sure. Nothing'll stop us having a good time." The screen door gave the sound of a bullfrog. She pulled him inside; they climbed narrow steps, the center of each one worn away, perhaps by the other men who had followed her up to her bed. She stopped him on the second floor, jingled through her purse, rattled a key into the lock and opened the door, leaving him in the hall. She took two high-heeled steps and pulled the rasping light string. "Well, come on in." She came and put her arms around his neck and, walking backwards, pulled him over the worn doorsill. Her thighs were soft. He could not embrace her because he still carried his cane and case. His face was enveloped again in the smell of alcohol. Her lips were fleshy. Hardie had told him to open his mouth; he opened his mouth. Her teeth were uneven, one being gold-covered and smoother than the others. Her body warmed his from his knees to shoulders. She pushed her thighs and stomach hard against him. He was embarrassed by what he knew she found there. "You don't waste no time, sweetness." She kissed him again lightly, then laughed. "Forgot to lock the door. This ain't no public function." She released him, closed and locked the door, then passed him, walking to the center of the room. It did not sound very large; there was no echo. The light string scraped against glass. "There. Now I can't see neither." She came to him, pushing against him, and kissed him. When at last she pulled away, his lips were wet, sticky with lipstick. "Undress me."

He had extended his hand before he realized he was still carrying his cane and case. He put them on the floor, the case falling against his ankle as he straightened up and reached for her with nervous, trembling hands. He hoped she could not see them.

The firmness of her ribs and back, covered with a padding of spongy flesh, came under his hand. Finding seven buttons, he undid them, his hands still shaking. She wiggled and his hands were shocked by an expanse of bare skin, moist and cool. Her bra strap circled her back like a barrel stave, flesh bulging on either side of it.

"Well, for God's sakes, sweetness, unhook it."

He pulled the bra strap tight and took the prongs from the eyes. The strap left ridges, designs on her skin. She turned suddenly and her breasts tickled his palms; unblemished but design-marked skin surrounded small cold nipples. In his stomach was the same deep, hollow feeling he had experienced at the bar when he had stroked her dress. He felt as if only his hands were really alive. He could feel only his hands and the inside of his stomach growing tight. She came close again, putting her arms around him, squeezing her breasts between them, the top of her dress bunched around her waist. "It as good as you thought, ain't it, Ludlow?"

She had asked that, he knew, because she could feel the frightened stiffness of his body, although she did not know he was frightened. She stepped away from him. "I'll finish it." Her shoes bumped across the wood floor. Elastic and material fluttered. "Now, I'll do you."

She took hold of his belt, unbuckled it and pulled his pants and undershorts over his hips, down his legs and onto the floor.

55

He stepped out of them. For an instant a memory came from long ago, of his mother doing the same thing. He could remember nothing else, not his mother's voice, or the feeling of her hands, just simply his clothes being pulled away.

Malveen's hands were on his shoulders, then pushing his jacket down his arms, her fingernails catching along his shirt sleeves. She slipped off his tie, unbuttoned and took off his shirt. Her hands touched his stomach, making it pull in as if from a blow. "Come on, man, what you waiting for?"

"Nothing, baby." He tried in vain to sound tough.

"The bed's over here." She pulled him across the room until he felt sheets against his knee. Then she giggled; she was still quite drunk. "You got your shoes and socks on. You planning to screw and run?"

He sat on the bed and unlaced his shoes, slipped off his socks. Under his bare buttocks the bed was unmade, rumpled, and he could not stop himself from thinking of the two other men who tonight had perhaps been sitting on that very spot.

"Come on, Ludlow." She was behind him on the bed. "Come on, sweetness. Love me to death."

He stretched out beside her. She had been sweating, but the sweat had dried. She was cool and sticky. She rubbed her feet against his, then forced her soft leg between his own stiff legs and upward. She kissed him and he kissed her back as Hardie had instructed. She began to moan under the kiss; it seemed unreal. He remembered Hardie or someone had told him that a girl would begin to moan, and he knew it must be time to make love to her. He rolled on top of her; she opened her legs. He was surprised how very far he could get into her. Then, before he really knew it, it was all over, faster even than his quiet, lonely moments with his thoughts and handkerchief, and he was weaker than he had ever been in his life.

Malveen, spread beneath him, was pushing at him and cursing. "You bastard! Is that all? You couldn't even hold your hot little rod!"

He did not understand. "What's wrong?"

"What's wrong! You mealymouthed mother-fucking little blind bastard! Get away from me, you fucking faggot! Get *off* me!"

In a tangle of sheets, he pushed himself off her and to his knees. "What'd I do, Malveen?"

"What did you do! I oughta make you pay. You didn't do nothing. Not a damn thing. I was just getting used to you. What did you do? Get your clothes and get out of here." The bedsprings crackled and lurched upward. The light chain pinged and something heavy and hard grazed his head and fell in front of him—his shoe. After that, kneeling on the bed, he was pelted with all his clothes, as she scurried around the room screaming at him. "Get out of here!"

Finally the barrage of clothes stopped and she dragged him off the bed, onto his feet, and pushed him across the room. The door banged open and she shoved him out into the hall, where other women giggled and whispered:

"Who that?"

"Malveen surely did tell his ass off."

"Didn't he pay her?"

"She called him a faggot."

His clothes hit his legs. "Get dressed and get away from my door. I don't want nobody to know I shamed myself." She went back into the room. "Here's your God damn cane." It clattered beside him. "And take this too!" There was a heavy thud in the mound of clothes. He bent to touch it and found his instrument case. "Now get out!" The door slammed.

To a chorus of giggles, razor-sharp whispers and clicking tongues, he dressed himself, untangling each piece of clothing from the pile at his feet. By the time he put on his jacket the women were gone, having disappeared one by one behind locking doors. He was alone in the hall. Behind Malveen's door it was quiet. He picked up his cane and case and crept down the steps, feeling as if the staircase was lined with finger-pointing women.

In the street, he asked the first person he met for directions, and started home. He had walked slowly for ten minutes before he realized his cheeks were wet with tears, not so much from shame as from anger. He vowed solemnly that nothing like that would ever happen to him again. He vowed too that one day he would return to Malveen's room and bed, and even if he had to pay her, he would prove himself. But then he began to doubt he would ever be able to keep either vow and became so deeply discouraged he had to stop. Finally he went on, and as he neared Missus Scott's, he was smiling. At least, he was thinking, he knew now what it was all about.

5

Eight hours later Ludlow, waking, first became aware of the cars and people in the street. He rolled over and placed his fingers on the face of his clock (an ordinary one with the glass removed), felt the time at one o'clock and climbed out of bed. Near the foot of the bed he found the balled-up handkerchief he had used the night before and, angry at himself for the first time about doing this, flung it away from him. That would not be enough any more.

He was not at all hungry and, being afraid of talking to anyone, fearing that by now everyone in the world would know what had happened with Malveen the night before, he remained in his room, sitting in the warm breeze that pushed through the window. He fingered his instrument, but during the next five hours, he did not often think of music as he hoped he would. Instead he reviewed many times what had happened, and what his life had been since he left the Home. Finally he thought he was beginning to understand it all:

59

Life outside the Home was exactly the same as it had been inside. The people on top of you would always try to keep you down; the people under you would always try to pull you down.

It was that simple. He had known this to be true inside the Home. His mistake had been to expect it to be different, better, outside. But it would not be better or different, ever. After he decided this, he began to feel less discouraged.

Just then, Etta-Sue Scott knocked. With his new discovery in mind, he opened the door.

"Mama say you always come down this time to eat. She worrying about you."

"She don't got to worry." He was already returning to the window. "I ain't hungry." He knew how he wanted it to sound, angry, and was surprised when it emerged very nearly that.

There was a long silence; though he had left the door open, she remained outside the room. When finally she spoke, something had gone out of her voice—pity or condescension perhaps —and she was nervous. "You eating out tonight?"

"I ain't eating at all tonight. I'm on a diet." That was better still. He realized quite suddenly why he had never been able to talk this way before; he had not believed it before.

"You don't look fat to me." She was completely serious.

"It my feet, from standing on them. I got flat, fat feet."

She hesitated for a moment, then giggled. "Oh, you fooling with me." She was not at all angry. "Flat, fat feet!" She stopped laughing. "You really ain't eating?"

"No. I ain't hungry." He spoke just a bit more savagely.

She fell silent once more. "Mister Washington? You ain't not eating because of me, is you?"

This surprised him. He could not decide whether or not to show that surprise. He answered with a question. "What'd you do?"

60

"Well . . . maybe I was kinda short with you yesterday." She stopped. Before he could comment, she went on: "It wasn't you at all. Mama and me had a fight before you come down. God, I'm almost twenty-two years old! I been away from home four years, off and on, but when I come back she always telling me what to do, like I don't know nothing." She came into the room, dragging her slippered feet. "She make me so mad! I don't want to get told what I got to do and when to do it. Like she said when you was there? That she didn't want me to go into where you work? Now suppose I just wanted to come and listen and maybe have a beer. For all she know, I'm a bad girl up in Willson City, which I ain't"—she was embarrassed just then—"but when I come down home, she treats me like some little kid."

Ludlow had listened to a particular tone in her voice, his head cocked toward her. This was not the first time a person he did not at all know had told him more than the person should have told, more than Ludlow wanted to know. It had happened several times in Boone's. The particular tone was that of a person talking to himself, not to Ludlow at all, as if the person were all alone, as if the blindness were not in Ludlow's eyes at all, did not keep Ludlow from seeing, but from being seen. Even after she stopped talking, he went on thinking. He did not realize she had stopped until she started again.

"So yesterday, I didn't mean to hurt your feelings or anything by being so short. I was just mad at Mama. So I wish you'd come down and eat if you really ain't got someplace to go." Her high voice almost broke under the weight of apology.

Ludlow's natural inclination was to forgive her, if indeed he had anything to forgive. But that would only erase the advantage he now held. "You didn't do nothing to me." He made it sound as if she had done a great deal and he was still angry at her. "I just ain't hungry."

She remained silent for a moment, then sucked her tongue. "All right." She scraped toward the door. "I'll tell Mama." She was sad. For an instant he wanted to stop and tell her he would eat with them after all, but he was afraid. Never again did he want to put himself in a position where he could so easily be humiliated, hurt or shamed. And that would surely happen if he gave anyone the chance. Her footsteps were cut short by the knock and click of the closing door.

Not long after that, at seven o'clock, Hardie called for him. Ludlow attacked him as soon as the trombone player stepped into the room. "You messed me up, you bastard."

Hardie's voice was smiling. "How?"

"With Malveen. You told it all wrong." With his fingers, he inspected the finished knot of his bow tie.

"What happened? Didn't she give you none?"

He half-lied. "She kicked me out in the hall with all my clothes off. I had to stand there dressing while a bunch of whores stood around giggling." Thinking of it now, he felt again his pain and embarrassment. This was not in his voice.

"No fooling? I wish I'da seen that."

"I wish it been *you!*"

"Me too. I'da risked that for a piece of her."

Ludlow did not know what to answer. He clicked his tongue as Hardie sometimes did.

"So you lost this time. Next time you win. Besides, you won't never make the same mistake again—whatever mistake you made." The bedsprings yawned under Hardie's voice; he was sitting now. "You can't win them all."

"I'm trying to win most of them." Ludlow was putting on his coat.

Hardie snorted. "Hell! Who ain't?"

Ludlow laughed. He did not really like to play a role with Hardie. Still, the way he felt about Hardie had changed. For the first time he felt himself to be Hardie's equal, and Hardie did not seem to mind.

When they arrived at Boone's, Small-Change ran up to him: "What'd you do to her, little boy?"

Ludlow went warm. Now they would all know about the night before, how it had really been. "What you mean?"

"Don't kid me, little boy. I met Malveen today and she say she working out of a better bar, where the fellows buy you more drinks. And I say, 'That's good. We can both work there.' And she say, 'No, we can't.' And I say, 'How come?' And she say, 'We can't, is all. Don't bother me.' But Small-Change is smart and wouldn't let her off that easy!" She sounded triumphant, almost happy. "So I kept at her. And finally she say she ain't working out of Boone's no more because of you. She hates your guts."

Ludlow remained calm; it was all he had left. "Why?"

"She say you treated her mean. What'd you do? She say you cheated her."

"I what?" He realized that if he did anything but ask questions he would expose and betray himself.

"You cheated her. She say you promised her something and then treated her mean." She was not angry. Curiosity alone excited her. "What'd you promise her?"

Before he spoke he took a very deep breath. "What's it to you, baby?"

"Nothing." She paused. "You a bad man, Ludlow Washington." There was admiration in her voice.

"Well, then you just stay out of my way." He did not need to breathe deeply this time.

PART THREE

INTERVIEW . . .

    So I was with Bud Rodney, but after a while I didn't like what he was making me play. I mean, I started to really listen to some things Norman Spencer was doing on piano—like breaking up time a little. He wasn't going boom-boom-boom-boom with both hands. He was going boom-boom-boom-boom with his left, but the right was going boom-da-boom-boom, da-da-boom-da, and like that. Of course, he wasn't one of us young boys. It was just his way because he was really an old-time player.

    Anyway, Rodney, he didn't like Norman Spencer's music at all and I was getting hot under the collar and thinking it was time to go to New York. And finally I did go.

I

He had just finished dressing. In the early evening coolness, a breeze blowing through his shirt and chilling his armpits, he sat by the window waiting for Hardie. After seven months he no longer needed Hardie to guide him to work (he knew the way within five steps), but still he looked forward to their walks to Boone's. He was closer to Hardie than to any person he had ever known.

The footsteps that stopped at his door were not Hardie's; they were Etta-Sue Scott's. She had been away in Willson City for the past four months, but had returned suddenly a few days before. She and Ludlow had not spoken.

She knocked. Without moving from the window, he told her to come in.

She did not greet him, simply began: "Your friend called— Hardie? He can't pick you up. You want me to take you over?"

"I can make it by myself." The patronizing tone in her voice annoyed him. He did not turn from the window.

Without closing the door, she came two steps into the room. "You sure?" He was certain that really she was asking if he could do anything at all by himself.

He turned on her. "Could you get around this house with your eyes closed? You know how many steps long the hall is?"

"No." There was weakness in her voice and he aimed for it.

"I been walking to Boone's every day for seven months. How dumb you think I am not to know the way?" The thought that she might think him dumb made him cruel. "Just what is your problem, Miss Scott? Why the hell you so all-the-time wrongways?"

She sighed and it surprised him. He had expected, had wanted even, an argument. He waited for her answer, but none came.

He went on: "I met you four months ago—right? I walk into the kitchen and right away you jumping salty like seven oceans. So then next day you come up here and apologize, telling me you wasn't mad at me; it was your mama. So I said to myself"—he was lying now—"that's a nice girl and we can be friends. So the next couple times I talk to you, I try to be your friend, but you just as salty. Now, let me ask you, what I done to you?" This time he would wait for an answer, even if it took hours.

She sighed again. "Nothing."

"Well, what? You think I'm trying to get inside your clothes?" Though he had conjured dreams about her, he had never wanted her seriously. But saying it, he discovered that, even though he knew only that she was tall and heavy, he really did want her after all. But that could wait for a moment.

"No. It ain't that. It's—" she stopped.

"What?"

"It all right if I sit down?" She did not wait for an answer; bedsprings wheezed under her weight. For an instant he felt himself lying on top of her, above wheezing springs. "It just this, Ludlow." Always before, she had called him Mister Washington. "I—don't know how to talk to you. I mean, you—blind and all and—and I don't want to say nothing that'd make you feel bad." She sighed. "But then I always do anyway."

"My being blind ain't no secret, Etta-Sue." He tried her first name. "You think I ain't noticed it?"

"It still hard." She whined a little.

"So now we both know I'm blind. What about the rest of it?" He was thinking about the contempt he was sure she felt for him, the place he worked and the people he worked with.

But she seemed genuinely puzzled. "What rest of it?"

"Okay. Maybe there ain't no rest." He realized that if he was to get her into his bed, he would have to change his tactics a bit, ease up on her. "All right, Etta-Sue. I understand. It could be real tough for someone like you, normal and all, being around me." He made himself smile. "So now we got it straight and we can be friends. All right?"

"All right, Ludlow." Her voice was the warmest he could remember. She got up, the bedsprings rattling, and again he imagined himself on top of her. "You sure you can make it to work by yourself?" The question came out differently.

"Sure, I can. You don't need to bother, thanks." He paused. "Remember when I asked you to come over to Boone's? Why don't you do that one of these nights before you go back. I'll get them to play your favorite song."

She answered flatly. "I ain't going back. I quit my job. You know how Mister-Charlie is. He think when you work for him, he owns you. My boss tried to . . . you know . . . touch me in the pantry." She was embarrassed. "So I had to quit."

Ludlow was amazed, though he concealed it. How different

she was from the girls he knew. Malveen or Small-Change would have given Mister-Charlie what he wanted—then charged him dearly for it. Ludlow did not really understand Etta-Sue's kind of girl. But that was not important. He knew now she would be in New Marsails for a good while. It would be a luxury to have a girl in the house where he lived.

"Well . . ." He got up and walked to the bed for his coat, wondering if she was looking at him. "Got to get moving. It was nice talking to you, Etta-Sue."

"Nice talking to you, Ludlow." She was near the door. "I'll run on downstairs." For some reason she was embarrassed, but said no more, simply closed the door behind her.

For a moment before he left for Boone's he stood thinking, his arm in one sleeve, the coat hanging at one side. He thought about coming home and Etta-Sue sneaking into his room, into his bed and them making love quietly so her mother would not wake up. He thought how nice it would be simply to pack his instrument and come home to his own girl.

Hardie, very excited, arrived at Boone's a few minutes after Ludlow. "Look, man, I got these two girls at a table over here. I was standing in the grocery store, opening a pack of cigarettes. So in they come and the one, Minnie, she sees the bread in cellophane and gets knocked out because she ain't never seen store-bought bread before. I knew they had to be country, real country! And they's both them big girls, with high asses and high little titties. So anyway I got them to come over with me."

Ludlow wanted to laugh, but deadpanned. "Which one you want to stick me with?"

"The smart one. I mean, neither of them all that smart. They real country! But one's just a little bit smarter. I think maybe she been outa the cotton field a little longer. Now you take her and be real Buster Brown and it'll be easy for you. Anyways, I bet she got the juicy box."

"Okay, man." They went through the smoke and talk and sat at a table. The smell of powder and perfume was very strong. Hardie introduced him. Ludlow's girl had a voice like a bugle: high, hard and straight. "I ain't never talked to no blind man before." She was too blunt to be true.

He would have to be gentle, humble and polite to disarm her. "I hope it don't make you feel funny, miss."

"Why should it? How'd it happen?"

"I was just born that way. Just God's will." He lowered his head. "God's will, is all."

"Maybe it was just something your mama ate."

Now Ludlow knew why Hardie had pushed her off on him. "I guess so." She was not going for the usual nonsense. He would have to find out more about her. "Why'd you come to New Marsails?"

"Did I got to have a reason to come?" She was the least bit defensive.

He made his voice gentle. "Of course you do. We all came for something—else we woulda stayed where we was." He waited. Her next answer would be important.

For an instant she was silent. Ice knocked in her glass. Then she laughed. "I wasn't about sitting up there waiting for my daddy to give me to some dirty sharecropping friend of his."

That was what had happened, what she had run from. He added to it. "And you ain't about to get taken in by the first smooth-talking city nigger you meet, thinking you just a dumb country girl."

She laughed. "That's right." She was not quite as hard now.

"Yeah. I understand what you saying. My daddy was a

72

preacher and didn't think I could be nothing but a beggar or something. I had to get out his house and show him." He shook his head. "I guess blind folks and girls got something in common —people don't give us much credit. Blind folks is only good for sitting on a corner with a tin cup. Girls is only good for filling a bed." He paused for effect. "But we human too and want all the things strong men want."

There was silence, but Ludlow felt sure he had reached her. He could sit back and wait now. Taking her home would be her idea.

"Say, Ludlow?" Hardie was leaning forward, his voice low and close. "Rodney giving us the sign."

He nodded, turned back to the girl. "Well, I hope you be around. It really nice talking to you."

"We be sitting right here." She tried to sound seductive.

Rodney called for a ballad that had been very popular thirteen years before. They had never played it as a group, though all the men knew it. Ludlow stated the theme and took the first solo. For some reason, he felt happy and warm, and was puzzled by the feelings. Then he understood them. He felt himself sitting on the old porch, a little boy. In the house behind him the radio played the song. His mother's footsteps came out of the house and then her hand rested on his head. The heat was going down and in the back yard his sister, with friends, was giggling.

He finished his solo and backed to the piano.

"What the hell that supposed to be?"

"What was what supposed to be, Mister Rodney?"

"You call that music?" He said nothing more.

Ludlow did not understand what Rodney was talking about. When the set was finished and he and Hardie were coming off stage, he asked.

"The ballad?" Hardie sucked his tongue. "I don't know. I heard it, man, but I couldn't tell you what you was doing. You wasn't even in time sometimes, you know, like Norman Spencer? Hell, man, I can't tell you." Hardie was perplexed. "Let's get back to the table."

Ludlow shook his head. "She won't take no pushing. Leave me at the bar. Come get me in about five minutes."

"You cut me into pieces!" Hardie guided him to the bar.

"I don't want to cut into you at all." The bar pressed against his stomach.

Hardie's laughter blended with the other laughter in the café.

All at once he felt empty and sad. He realized he did not want to go back to the table, to that girl. But he had no idea what he would rather do. Perhaps it was the song they had played. He had very little memory of his life before the Home and it bothered him that from time to time, when he did remember something, it was not when he wanted to remember, but only when he was re-minded of those times. And afterward it always made him sad, because he could never hold onto the feeling of the memory.

He began to think about Etta-Sue Scott. Not that she made him feel any better, but at least with her—and he did not doubt he would have her—it would be something different, maybe some-thing steady, at least as steady as he wanted it to be. He tried to imagine how she would be, but could not. She was too different from the other girls to whom he had made love. She might not even be very good. But at least she would not be the same old thing, like the girl at the table.

"Ready?" Hardie was at his shoulder. "She been asking for you about twice a minute."

Ludlow shrugged, then chuckled. "Well, lead me to the hole and let's see if I can plug it."

74

2

He could not bring himself to stay with the girl more than a few hours. He had known he would feel this way even before she suggested the four of them go to her room for a drink, and so he had taken care to remember the number of steps and turns from Boone's to her house. After Hardie and his girl left them, Ludlow did his duty—he felt it to be just that—and left as soon as possible, making some excuse when she asked him from bed to spend the day with her. He got home at nine in the morning, tried to sleep but could not, and finally at eleven, sadness making him restless, got up and dressed.

He practiced and this made him feel a little better. He tried to recall phrases, melodies, that would in turn help him to remember what he had done with the ballad the night before.

After a while even practicing did not help his sadness, restlessness, and he began to wonder what Etta-Sue Scott was doing. He tried to think of a good reason to go downstairs, and finally remembered that Missus Scott had once told him that if ever he had something to read that was not in Braille, she would try her best to read it to him. In his closet his hands found a music book with a chapter about the muscles of the mouth that were involved in producing a certain tone (something he had learned several months before, Hardie having read the chapter to him) and started downstairs.

Missus Scott was not even home; Etta-Sue was alone in the kitchen cooking a ham. He pretended he did not want to disturb her, but she insisted warmly that he sit down and tell her what he wanted. "After all, ain't we friends?" By the way she spoke, Ludlow knew friendship was all she had in mind. She had not returned to her previous attitude toward him, but he recognized the tone in her voice as that of a mother, very like Missus Scott's.

He told her why he had come down, at the same time deciding he would proceed slowly. He sensed she might be thinking about her being twenty-one and his being younger. He could afford to let her think it for a while.

"I can read that for you." She was at the stove. "Just wait until I get this ham set right."

He waited quietly, surrounded by the sounds of the kitchen, which he loved: the water roaring in the kettle, the ham's fat dripping and sizzling, the knockings and bangings and stirrings. These sounds never changed. He imagined, though he did not know for certain, his mother's kitchen must have sounded like this.

Finally she put down a large fork or spoon and pulled out the chair across the table from him. "Let's see that."

He handed across the book. She fanned the pages and began to read. He did not listen to the words, only to her voice, high and tight. Most of the other voices he knew had been loosened by liquor or confidence. She cleared her throat a good deal, as if the tightness was caused not by what she was, but rather by a small bone or ball of dust. When she was finished, she closed the book and sighed. "I didn't understand a word." She paused a moment. "What this larynx anyways?"

"It makes your voice."

She sighed again, impressed. "I bet you know as much about that thing as a doctor."

He shrugged. This was good; the more impressed she was with him, the sooner she would forget about her being older. But she had not yet forgotten. "You really only sixteen, Ludlow?" He nodded. "My, you just a baby." She was teasing. He did not like it, but had to hide his dislike. If she realized she was reaching him, he would be giving truth to her statement.

"I guess so. And you an old lady of twenty-one." He decided, smiling, to do some teasing of his own. "How come you ain't married and got seven kids?"

There was silence from across the table. He sniffed burning sugar, fat, cloves. Then: "I almost was." She went no further.

He added another touch. "Well, twenty-one ain't all that old."

"No, I guess not." Then her voice came alive again. "There a lot of bad women in where you work?" He nodded. "How old's they?"

"No telling. They anywheres from sixteen to thirty."

"I see them sometimes and they look older."

"That's because of what they seen, Etta-Sue. You ain't seen what they seen."

"I ain't even seen what you seen." She paused, choked on her next words to him. "I mean—I'm sor—" She was embarrassed.

"That's all right, Etta-Sue. I do see it, in a way." He reached

77

out, found the book in the middle of the table, and dug his finger-nail between the pages.

"Like what?" She leaned forward, her elbows squeaking on the oilcloth.

He was trying hard to keep his mind on the reason he was talking to her at all, trying to continue controlling the conversation, but she seemed so interested and earnest, he found he liked talking to her. "What you see, only more. I mean, you colored too and we all live together, the whores and the ministers. We that close." He held up two fingers. "But down at Boone's, ain't no ministers. Everybody got a deal going."

"You don't trust nobody, do you." It was not a question.

"No, ma'am!"

"What about your friend Hardie?"

"I don't need to trust him. That ain't part of our friendship."

"In church they always say you got to love and trust people. I mean, that in church, but still it kind of true. I mean, I think so."

"Look, Etta-Sue, me and Hardie agree on two things." He tallied them on his fingers, enjoying talking like this. "One—he don't trust me and I don't trust him. So we got that straight between us, and that way nobody's asking nothing of anybody, and that way ain't nobody getting let down. Two—he know I'm smart and I know he smart, so neither of us trying to pull nothing. It won't pay. It won't work. So we living in peace, and if we living in peace, we might as well be friends."

"What happens when you meet a girl and want to get married?"

He did not have an answer, had never considered it, and it stopped him. But if he knew anything at all, it was to answer quickly. "Maybe I won't never get married because maybe the way I feel won't be good in a marriage." That would hold her, and if he understood her at all, it might work for him.

"We all getting married someday. Even me."

She was telling him, whether or not she knew it, that she had once been hurt. He made his voice very tender. "What was it happened to you, Etta-Sue? If you can tell me."

She was silent again, longer this time. "Oh, it ain't unusual."

He did not want to push her. But he did want to give the impression he cared deeply. "It musta been hard on you."

"Maybe." She was sad now. If he could cheer her up, it would be a point for him.

"You know, when my daddy left me at the Home"—he sat back in his chair—"I thought I'd cry for a year. I cried and cried. And finally I didn't cry no more. And it all turned out good." As he spoke of this for the first time in years, he had a sudden feeling of sadness. He swallowed it. He had no time now to be sad. "Because if he didn't left me at the Home I woulda never been a musician and I'd be on somebody's corner with a cup. So things come right after all."

"Maybe they do." He thought she sounded better.

He went on, trying something new. "Look, why don't you come by Boone's tonight. I mean, it always happy at Boone's and like I told you, I'll get them to play your favorite song. What's it anyways?"

"Mine?" She seemed surprised and shy. "Oh, I don't know."

"Come on. Sure you do."

"Well, okay. It *That Won't Happen to Me.*"

"No fooling?" It was a standard bluesy-type song, which had been made popular several years before by Inez Cunningham. Now most female singers had it in their acts. The words were sad, bitter and defiant. "We play that sometimes. You could come by tonight and I'll have them play it. I promise." He was trying to sound just the slightest bit innocent and young now. It would make her more secure.

"All right." He could not tell if she was actually going to come.

"You ain't just talking now?"

"Well . . ." She was uncertain. "Yes, all right, I'll come—if I can get out the house without Mama knowing."

"She won't mind. She likes me. Tell her you just coming to hear me."

She laughed, still shy. "Well, I'll try."

"It'll be all right and you'll have fun." He was thinking too that he might have to put a few drinks into her, not enough to get her drunk, just enough to allow her to consider some possibilities. "Promise you'll come." He might have been pushing too hard, a mistake.

The mother's tone returned to her voice. But she sighed and he still was not certain what was going to happen that night. "We'll see."

3

He had played five sets and there was still no sign of her. It was quarter to one. If she had been coming at all, she would have arrived already. He and Hardie had just descended the steps of the stage, had just reached the bar. "What's wrong, man?" Hardie put his arm around Ludlow's shoulder.

"Why should anything be wrong? I wish that bastard Rodney would let me drink." He was fed up with standing at the bar empty-handed. He would speak to Rodney about it, would refuse to play if Rodney did not let him drink.

"Come on, man. You talking to Hardie, your nigger. It was in your music. You didn't play that last song, you jumped on it with both feet and stomped it to death." Hardie's arm left his shoulder; where the arm had rested he had begun to sweat.

He would not whine to Hardie about it. It was not Hardie's business anyway.

"We all got them bad days, Ludlow. Look, I got a girl coming in here. Maybe she got a sister or friend she can call. We'll get a bottle and have some good times."

He would not even whine to himself. It made little difference whether or not she came. But he had been certain he had made progress with her. It was a blow to his pride to discover he had not.

Hardie had continued to talk about his girl and her possible friend. "Come on. What you say?"

"I'm tired. I'm going home to sleep—for once." He could not bring himself to run with Hardie tonight.

There was a shrug in Hardie's voice. "Okay. Got to get some sleep sometime, I guess." They were silent for the remainder of the break.

At one, back on the stage, his instrument to his lips, caring not at all whether Rodney approved, Ludlow tried some new things he had been practicing. If Rodney said anything, Ludlow would tell him to fire him. He knew now he was the best on his instrument in the entire city. He would tell Rodney, "Go on, old man, send me back to the Home. In a year I'll get out and take your job away." Besides, he was not trying the new things only because he was mad at Etta-Sue. He had been getting tired of the music Rodney forced him to play. He wondered sometimes how it would have been if he had been able to go with Inez Cunningham and if he would have met Norman Spencer, who refused to work anywhere but in one night club in Harlem, New York. He would wait one more year—he had to—and then he would telegram Inez Cunningham to see if she still wanted him.

When the set was finished, Rodney said nothing to him and he went back to the bar.

For an instant he thought the hand which gripped his elbow belonged to a man. "I made it." Her voice was strangely young, excited. "I almost made it without her catching me, but she woke up and tried to stop me and I told her I was coming anyways. So, here I am."

He was relieved to know he had not failed with her. "You have a big fight?"

"Wasn't no time. I just marched right out the house." She stopped, then her voice was closer to his ear. "Can I have a drink, please?"

"Why, sure." He was surprised. He had thought he might have trouble. He raised his hand, waited for the bartender to come and ordered. "And one for me too."

The bartender reminded him of Rodney's instructions.

He leaned across the bar and whispered. "Listen, man, I'm sick of this shit. I'm bringing people into this bar and you know it. You tell Rodney if I don't drink when I want to, I don't play when he wants me to. And tell him he can send me back to the Home if he want. I ain't afraid of him no more."

The bartender replied that Ludlow did not have to bare so many teeth, and went for the drinks. Ludlow turned back to Etta-Sue and smiled, hoping she had not heard the conversation. But if she had and made no remark, he must be making progress with her.

"Is they, you know, prostitutes?" She must have been looking around the bar now.

"Where?"

"I'm sorry, Ludlow." She sounded nervous.

"Listen, Etta-Sue, you got to stop that."

She hesitated, then went on, "Over at the table in the corner." She described four girls, Small-Change among them.

"Yes, they whores, Etta-Sue."

"They really do look good! Got such nice clothes."

"Them's part of their business expenses." He smiled. Out of her mother's kitchen, she was certainly a different person.

She had laughed at his joke. "How much they make a week?"

"Why?" He paused. "You going into business?"

"Who, me?" She laughed again, a better laugh than before. "You think I could?"

"I don't know what you look like. Tell me."

This laugh was an embarrassed one. "How can I tell you?"

"Go on."

"Well, I'm too tall, five feet ten. I weigh a hundred fifty and I'm not very curvy. I think my legs is good. I mean, I don't got skinny legs like some women do, and, well, my—oh, I can't tell you about them. But I guess I'm a little lighter than you. I don't like my color much. . . . I don't know how to tell you about my face."

"I'll tell that myself." He reached out before she could protest (if she was going to) and put his hand on her face, not a bad one at all. He could feel the things she had gotten from her mother. Her cheeks were broad, set wide apart. Her nose was a small ball with good-sized nostrils. Her eyes were set deeper than her mother's, her lips not as thick and much softer. "You didn't say what color hair you got."

"Guess." She was becoming playful.

"Green." They had taught him a little about color in the Home.

"It bright red. I don't know where it come from. Some Irishman in my past." She laughed. The bartender had brought their drinks while she had been talking and now they sipped at them. This was not Ludlow's first drink, but it was his first one in Boone's, and it meant something to him. He enjoyed it.

"You planning to tell me the name of this lovely creature, Ludlow?" It was Hardie, clapping his shoulder.

"I don't know. You dangerous." He paused. "Etta-Sue, this Otis Hardie."

"Pleased to meet you." Hardie was being formal.

Etta-Sue did not reply. Ludlow hoped she was not impressed by Hardie.

"Don't she talk?" Hardie turned to him again.

"Yeah, but only to me."

Etta-Sue laughed. "I'm pleased to meet you, Mister Hardie." She had not been impressed; Ludlow could tell from her voice.

"Just Hardie, baby. Ain't no Mister needed." He paused. "Hey, Ludlow, it that time again. Etta-Sue can sit with my girl while we playing."

"You want to do that?" He touched her arm; she drew back slightly.

"Sure."

Etta-Sue and Hardie left him at the bar. He was no longer confused by the change in her, just interested in it. That morning at home she had been an old woman—only twenty-one, but still a tired, sad, old woman. And now she had appeared, seeming so young, so completely different. He felt years older than she was. Perhaps it was being in Boone's, coming into Ludlow's world, that intimidated her, made her feel out of place and young.

"Where'd you ever find Snow White?" Hardie was back. "I heard of picking fruit before it ripe, but I ain't never heard of nobody eating the seeds!"

"She my landlady's daughter."

"Thought I seen her someplace. But, man, even though she look all right, I didn't know you was that far behind in your rent."

"Come on, nigger, let's play." Ludlow took a step toward the sound of Rodney's piano. On stage, he stopped beside it. "Hey, Mister Rodney, how about playing *That Won't Happen to Me?*"

"You drinking now, huh? And experimenting? And now you picking the numbers too? Why don't you just get yourself another piano player?"

Ludlow started to say he would consider it. But it was an important part of his plan to play Etta-Sue's favorite song; he pretended humility. "Okay, Mister Rodney, you right. Look, I'm almost seventeen and I just want a drink now and then, when it get hot in here. Now that's okay, ain't it?"

Rodney pounded a few chords. "Yeah, I guess so."

Ludlow realized that indeed Rodney did not want to lose him. Still he did not push. "Listen, Mister Rodney, I got my landlady's daughter over there. You know, trying to save a little rent? Her favorite song *That Won't Happen to Me*. So let's play it. It a good song. We played it before." He hated fawning to Rodney, but it was the best way. In a year and four months he would spit in his face.

"We'll play it toward the end."

"Thanks a lot, Mister Rodney." He even bowed slightly.

"But I don't want no more experimenting. I ain't no dope. I can hear that Norman Spencer in there."

"All right, Mister Rodney." He found his instrument on top of the piano.

They had played a good many numbers before Rodney finally called for Etta-Sue's number. After the set she told Ludlow he had played it beautifully. He was anxious now to discover if her description of her body was correct.

During the breaks of the next two sets, he and Etta-Sue talked and joked. She loosened up all during that time. She had four drinks and Ludlow knew if ever he was going to catch her, it would be tonight. What he had to decide was where. Her room was too close to her mother's. His room was on the third floor and he did not know if he could even lure her there. Of course he could somehow get her to Hardie's room, which would not be in use tonight, Hardie having found another bed to sleep in. But he was fairly certain she had not progressed that far. In fact, she might still balk at the entire idea. It would have to be his room, he decided, and he would have to be very careful.

They walked home arm in arm and, as quietly as possible, let themselves into the house. At the foot of the steps they stood, whispering. "I'm glad you come by, Etta-Sue." He tried to sound sincere. "But I hope you don't get in no trouble."

"It about time I did, don't you think?"

He wondered how she meant that. "I don't know. I mean, trouble with your mama is always bad trouble." He had been trying all the way home to think of some way to ease her upstairs almost without her knowing it, but now decided he would bring it into the open, though he would disguise his intentions. "Look, Etta-Sue, if you don't want to go right to sleep, we can have a nightcap." He did not make it sound serious. "I got a bottle in my room. I can go upstairs and bring it down if you want."

"You got a bottle in your room?" She giggled. "Ooo-eee! If Mama only knew that."

"You won't tell her, will you?" He knew already she would not. In her mind, she and Ludlow were allied against her mother.

"No. Yes, I'd like that. I had too much fun tonight just to go to sleep. Come on, we'll sneak up."

"You sure you want to come up? I mean, your mama might get real—"

"Hell with Mama!"

They climbed squeaking stairs to his room. Ludlow wondered what she expected to happen in his room—a friendly drink, or more. She went in ahead of him. "Where's the light, Ludlow?"

He did not know, had never used it. "Maybe it by the door."

"I found it." She sounded happy.

He closed the door, put his case and cane on the bed. "That bottle's in the dresser." He walked to it, opened the bottom drawer, pushed aside some shirts, produced the bottle, and shook it to find out how much remained. He did not drink a great deal and, though he had bought it three weeks before, it was still over three-quarters full. "We can have ourselves a nice little party." He waited to discover how that would go over. She remained silent.

Then: "You don't think Mama heard, do you? She probably laying wait for me."

"She didn't hear nothing except maybe just me going up to my room. If she awake, which she ain't, she probably thinks you still out." He could not let her get frightened now.

She walked to the bed and sat down heavily, jangling the springs.

He had to get her mind off her mother. "You have a good time tonight?"

"Oh yes! Everybody was so nice." Her joy lasted only a second.

He found two glasses on top of the dresser and poured the drinks, guiding the neck of the bottle with his fingers, then came to the bed, extending her glass. "Here's hoping you always have good times."

She did not reply, only swallowed, gasping.

"You worried, Etta-Sue?" This was going very badly. He was certain that if now he made a move toward her she would run. "Come on. Don't worry."

Still there was silence.

"Did I do something?" He tried everything.

88

"No. You been wonderful." She did not go on; her voice was tightening, a bad sign.

He came closer to the bed and squatted in front of her. "Come on, don't worry. It'll be all right tomorrow between you and your mama." To himself he cursed her mother now.

There was another silence. He waited for her to speak, listening to her breathing. She sighed finally; the bedsprings crackled as she shifted. Then she kissed him. He was stunned, had not at all been expecting it, did not understand why she had done it at that moment or, indeed, at all. Taking advantage of his opportunity, he kissed her, thinking that surely this was what he had wanted, had worked for. He realized too that during that last long silence she must have been deciding to kiss him.

He put down his glass, took hers and put it on the floor, grabbed her shoulders and kissed her again. She opened her mouth. He ran his hands down her arms, which were bare, jumped his hands to her sides, ribs, then placed his thumbs on her breasts, which were bigger, heavier than he had imagined—like Malveen's, but much harder. The nipples were flattened like cloth-covered buttons under a tight-fitting bra and a cotton dress.

He ended the kiss and she sighed his name. This was the only word she spoke as he undressed her, found the light, clicked it, came back to her, kissed her breasts, put his cane and case on the floor, pulled down the bedspread, helped her under the covers, undressed himself and joined her.

Her hips and back were broad. Her waist, as she had said, was not small, but she was not as fat as he had imagined from listening to her walk. She was simply big, and very solid.

Except for her arms, which she wrapped tightly around him, she lay perfectly rigid. He worked over her, trying everything he had learned in the past months, but still she did not move. Finally, just after he pushed inside her, he asked her if she knew, if she could tell him when she was getting close to the end.

"No." She was embarrassed. "I never got nowhere near the end."

He thought for a second. This was new to him. He would have to tell her exactly what to do, what to expect her body to feel. "It all right, Etta-Sue." He braced his feet against the footboard and started to move. "Don't worry. I'll tell you when."

4

Half an hour later, just as he began sliding into a doze, she sat up and clutched his arm. "You don't think Mama heard, do you?"

He rolled onto his back, found her breast and cupped it in his hand. "We didn't make no noise."

She turned toward him under his hand, not seeming to notice it. "I mean, heard us come up here?"

"Then she woulda been up here herself by this time." He slipped his arm around her, pulled her down and kissed her. "Come on, Etta-Sue, don't worry." All this annoyed him. She was already naked, in his bed. It was over now.

"But if she heard, she'd toss me out—and you too." She was lying close to him, her body rigid again.

He stroked her buttocks. Like her entire body, they were solid. "I ain't worrying." He wanted to get some sleep now.

She pushed even closer against him, hugging his waist. "How'd this happen, Ludlow?"

He tried hard to sound tender and gave her the usual answer. "When two people like each other, they don't ask how it happen. They just enjoy liking each other. What you getting all upset about? Didn't you like it?"

"Oh, yes." She squeezed him; she was strong. "I loved it. You so nice to me."

"Well, there. That must mean something." After he had told her what to do, she had worked out fine. Finally he had gotten it just the way he wanted it.

"I guess it do. But I'm worried about Mama. What time is it? It already getting light."

"There's a clock on the table." He sighed, yawned.

"Oh God! It quarter past six." She sat up again and, before he could catch her, was out of bed and dressing.

He decided not to stop her. She was getting on his nerves. "Don't go, Etta-Sue."

She bumped to her knees, must have been searching for something. Her voice, muffled, came from under the bed. "I got to get downstairs in my own bed. Mama wakes up around seven." She stood up.

He nodded. "I guess you right, but I don't like it."

She was dressed and out of his room in two more minutes, pausing only an instant to bend and kiss him.

He listened, but there was no sound from the stairs. He got up, opened the door and waited, listening, for five minutes. She must have made it safely. He nodded and smiled. As long as he was careful, this good situation would continue. He fell asleep, as proud of himself as he had ever been.

She was back in his room at two that afternoon, crying. "She called me all kinds of names and asked me where I been." Crying made her voice even higher, and a bit hoarse and she sounded as if someone was sticking one very sharp needle into the small of her back.

He had not realized there would be so many complications. He had never imagined that any girl would suffer such anguish over something so simple. "What you tell her?"

"That first I went to hear you and then I walked around, thinking. I said you wanted to bring me home but I just wanted to walk." She was sitting on his bed, crying. He was beside her, trying not to reach for her breast. She was not ready for that yet.

"She believe you?"

Her voice was small. "I think so."

"Well, then, don't worry." He put his arm around her shoulder. She did not move. "You sorry about last night?"

"Oh no. You was so nice to me." She leaned against him, but in a second pulled away and straightened up again. "But Mama was so mad."

He had not realized parents could be so much trouble. He could barely remember his own, and all of the people at Boone's had long since left theirs behind them. He turned to her and grabbed her shoulders. "Nice as your mama is, you grown now and got to live your own life. You can't let her tell you how to live." He hoped she would accept this; it would be too much trouble to go through something like this each time he made love to her.

"You really like Mama?"

"Sure I do. She been very nice to me." This was true. "And you like her too. That your problem. It just that she don't understand you. She thinks you still a little girl and you ain't."

"No. I ain't."

Now he could kiss her, and did. He wanted her before he

went to work, but he had to find out where her mother was. Etta-Sue probably would not have come to his room unless her mother was out, but he had to make certain. "Look, if you want, I'll talk to your mama for you. She downstairs?" He pretended to start to get up.

Etta-Sue caught his wrist. "She went shopping."

He put his arm around her waist, moved it up just under her breast, and kissed her. "I'll talk to her when she come back." He kissed her again, pushed her down onto the bed and crawled on top of her. She put her arms around his neck and opened her legs. He dropped between them. He did not even bother to take off her dress, only her underpants, pulling the dress up around her waist while she arched her back. He pushed his pants down around his ankles. This time he hardly had to tell her what to do.

Afterward they lay on his bed, her arms around him, his head on her breasts. It was different with her and he liked it, not just because she was different from the other girls he had made love to, but because she made him feel different. The others had not all been prostitutes—only Malveen—but there had been no feeling of permanence with them as there was with Etta-Sue. He remembered, when he had followed Malveen up the stairs to her room that night, that first time, he had wondered how many other men had followed her up those stairs. It was the same with the other girls. He always knew that the next night they might be with another man and that idea saddened him. It had been great fun at the beginning, but later it had become a chore. With Etta-Sue he knew he would be the only one for as long as he wanted her.

"You hungry, Ludlow?" She rubbed her hands over his back.

"A little." He smiled. This kind of concern was a luxury.

"I'll fix you something to eat if you want." She kissed the top of his head. She was really quite nice. He liked her.

"Okay." He got to his knees, kissed her and stood up.

"Where'd you put my underpants?"

"I don't know." He smiled. "Maybe they under you."

She giggled. "I got them." They rolled up her legs, snapping like rubber bands. "You can't walk around without no underpants." She was joking and it pleased him.

She asked to use his comb and brush, received permission, and when she was ready they went down to the kitchen. He sat at the table as she scurried around the room, preparing something for him. "I like fixing things for you."

"I'm glad." For some reason he felt suddenly uneasy, but dismissed it, deciding it was simply that any moment her mother would appear and they would have to pretend they hardly knew each other. He had done a good deal of lying to get things he wanted, but lying about things he already possessed was new to him, and somehow worse.

She brought some sandwiches to the table and sat across from him, remaining silent for a time. Then: "I want to tell you something."

He spoke through a mouth stuffed with tuna fish, bread, lettuce, and mayonnaise. "Sure, go on."

"It about the boy I was planning to marry." She stopped, as if expecting him to speak. He did not want to know about the other men in her life, and wondered why she wanted to tell him anyway. It was none of his business.

Finally she went on. "Not about why we broke up or anything, but about, you know, being close with him."

At first he did not understand her, but as she continued, it became clear what she was talking about.

"I only done it with him, only him."

He finished the sandwiches and rested his hands on the table. First her fingers touched his, then, timidly, as if expecting to be slapped, her hand crept over his.

"And I only done it with him seven times."

This was ridiculous. No girl he knew kept count, except the prostitutes and with them it was a matter of money.

She squeezed his hand. "I just want you to know that."

He nodded, not knowing what to say, what she wanted him to say.

"You believe me, don't you?" She sounded just the slightest bit desperate.

"Sure, Etta-Sue. It all right."

Far away, the lock on the front door clicked. Etta-Sue jumped, pulling her hand away; she leaned close, speaking in a terrified whisper. "It Mama. She home."

"I know." He remembered he had promised to speak to her mother. "Don't worry."

Etta-Sue stood up and rushed to the stove.

Missus Scott's footsteps, more tired and heavy than usual, came down the hallway. "That you, Etta-Sue?"

"Yes, Mama." Her voice shook.

The footsteps reached the doorsill. "How do, Missus Scott." Ludlow smiled and turned toward the door.

"Ludlow." She did not like him at all today.

It was best that he start talking immediately. "Hey, listen, Missus Scott, I come down to tell you about last night. I mean, Boone's a rough place, but nobody bothers the musicians' friends. Etta-Sue was feeling sad and I was talking to her and said for her to come on over. I didn't know you'd mind if she was with me." He stopped, wanting to know just how angry she was.

He followed her footsteps into the kitchen, to the counter, where heavy wrapping paper crackled. Then the chair where Etta-Sue had been sitting scraped back from the table and bumped forward again. "I just don't want her in places like that, Ludlow. It ain't fitting."

"Sure, Missus Scott, I understand you. But she was with me and I figured—"

"Why didn't you bring her on home?"

"You raised her decent, Missus Scott, so you don't got to worry. She just wanted to be alone. I mean, she didn't run off or nothing. She come home. But I know sometimes when I got to think things out I walk around. I mean, she told me you had a fight and that ain't good. And she just wanted to cool down a little bit. She wasn't doing nothing bad." That ought to have been good enough, but he had to wait.

"And nothing happened?" She was suspicious.

"Not a thing, Missus Scott. She sat with my friend's girl and listened, was all. And we talked when I wasn't playing."

Missus Scott fell silent. Ludlow was fairly certain now he had succeeded in calming her.

"Was you really so troubled, honey?" Missus Scott's voice had become quite tender.

"Yes, Mama." She paused. "I don't like to fight with you. It just that sometime you don't understand I'm grown now and got to live my own life."

Ludlow almost burst out laughing; she had paraphrased him almost exactly.

"Maybe you right, honey." Missus Scott was sad, but only for a second. "But now we know it and it'll be all right."

Etta-Sue rushed across the room and Ludlow listened to the pop of the kiss she placed on her mother's cheek. It made him feel odd, lonely. He had never known this kind of love.

"Mama? Mama, since Ludlow made everything all right can't we celebrate and have him to dinner?"

"That a good idea." Missus Scott's hand took his. "He a good, decent boy."

5

For the next two months it went on. Whenever her mother left the house for an hour or more, Etta-Sue would come to his room and they would make love. Sometimes she would come to Boone's to listen to him and then they would spend the night together, until she told him the sky was graying and she would have to go down to her own bed. Most nights she would stay at home and meet him in his room when he finished work. She fixed his meals, cleaned his room and saw to it his clothes were sent to the laundry. Ludlow basked in her attentions. He had never realized that devoting all his energy to one girl could pay off so well. He rushed home to her, leaving Hardie with various extra girls on his hands until the trombone player no longer bothered to arrange things for him.

If Missus Scott knew there was anything between Etta-Sue and Ludlow, she gave no hint. She was happy that her daughter seemed content at home and did not care why.

Ludlow did not realize he was thinking at all about marrying

Etta-Sue or anything close to it until one night, talking to Hardie during a break, he surprised even himself by blurting, "What you think being married is like?"

Hardie was close to shouting. "Are you listening to yourself?" He took a swallow, finishing his drink and called immediately for another. "Don't never mention that word when I'm around. It scares me." He waited until his drink came before he went on. "You really thinking about hanging yourself?"

Ludlow shrugged. He did not know why he had brought up the matter and wished he had not done so. "Well, I just wondering."

"When you just wondering, you is already gone and can't be drug back, even in chains." He stopped. "Who? Snow White?" After the first meeting, Hardie had called Etta-Sue nothing else; at times this annoyed Ludlow.

Ludlow nodded.

"Little miss daytime worker got you to see the light, huh?" Ludlow was not sure he liked Hardie's way of teasing him. It must have registered on his face because suddenly Hardie was quite serious. "Getting married all right, man, but you got to know the girl's with you. Understand me?"

Ludlow was not sure he loved Etta-Sue because he was not sure he knew what love was. He did know that in the last two months, making love to her, talking to her, sitting with her in the kitchen, he had felt less empty than ever before. He thought vaguely that the emotions he was now experiencing must be like those he had once felt for his family, for his mother, although any real, lasting memory of those emotions had long since been driven out of him. He had ceased to think of Etta-Sue as just another girl to whom he made love, but as something else, though he was not at all sure what.

"Do you understand me?" Hardie asked again.

"I understand. I mean, I like to be with her. You been seeing me run out of here soon as I can. I'm getting home to be with her."

Hardie was silent for a moment. Behind him, the bartender talked to a numbers man who was having a hard time keeping the police out of his life. Finally: "That ain't exactly what I'm talking about." He hesitated. "I mean, do she like what you doing? The daytime workers, they different. You, me, all the whores, Rodney even, we all nighttime workers. The daytime workers don't mind coming here once in a while, but pretty soon they start yawning and go on home. I mean, you blind and I ain't, but I don't get to see the sun any much more than you do. But that's the way I like it. And you do too."

"So?" Hardie was making him uncomfortable; he had wondered about these things himself.

"So—make sure she likes you working at night, and at Boone's, not just don't mind it—even that ain't enough—but that she really wants you to do it." He paused, then chuckled. "But whatever you do, man, good luck." He gripped Ludlow's elbow, but only for an instant.

Ludlow did not answer; in his head he was listening again to Hardie's advice. Somehow he would have to find out how Etta-Sue felt about this. He would have to do it without her realizing, because he was wise enough about women to know that once he had mentioned marriage to her, it could lead only to the actual marriage or to a breakup. All this was too good to lose by not being careful.

She was waiting in his room, asleep in his bed when he got home. Her breathing stood out clearly above the slight traffic running below the window. She did not wake up until he had undressed and climbed beside her.

She put her arms around his neck. "Hello." She was on her back.

"How long you been up here?" He rested his head on her shoulder, put his hand on her stomach, over her navel.

"Since three. When I was sure Mama was asleep." She turned onto her side and pulled herself in close to him. "How was you tonight?"

"Okay." He had not been thinking too much about music lately, but he was good enough so that no one seemed to complain.

"I missed you." She held him tighter and kissed him.

His mind was not on the kiss; he was still thinking about what Hardie had said, but even so he could feel himself beginning to want her. They had not made love since the night before.

"Etta-Sue, how come you ain't been to hear me play lately?" It was a clumsy beginning but vague enough for him to get away with it.

"You know how Mama is. She still don't like me going there, even with you looking after me." She pushed her knee gently between his legs. Her legs were warm, a bit sweaty.

"I was thinking maybe you didn't like Boone's. I mean, you a nice girl and maybe you don't like being in there with all them whores and con men." He tried not to let his body tense and give him away.

"Well . . . Boone's a real low-class place, but you won't be there long. You'll be starting your own band soon." This did not help him. He had told her of Rodney's hold on him, had shared with her his dream of starting a group of his own. "There anything wrong?"

He had decided to try another approach and her question gave him an opening. "I don't know for sure, but I'm thinking about quitting music."

"Oh, Ludlow, no." She seemed really surprised and, more important, unhappy.

"Like you say, Boone's a real low-class joint and it ain't a nice thing looking forward to playing in joints." For effect, he turned away from her.

She pursued him, pulled him back. "You can't do that!" She was sitting up, her voice coming down at him. "You don't even want to. I know you. All you got to do is just wait a year and then you'll start your own band, and a really good place, maybe even a white place'll hire you and then it'll be good. All you got to do is wait a year, one little year!"

Listening to her, he felt himself filling with real happiness. She did like his work and wanted him to continue doing it. He was glad he had talked to Hardie, because now he was certain. He turned back to her, held her tightly and kissed her, running his hand over her back, down to her buttocks. After a while, he rolled her onto her back.

They were married two Saturdays later. Hardie was his best man. Missus Scott did not object and, in fact, did not seem at all surprised.

6

He had been married five months. From time to time he felt bound by it—as on those occasions when Hardie introduced him to his current girl (they changed almost daily) and Ludlow got the scent of a new perfume or powder or just plain woman, or when, moving through the crowd at Boone's, a soft breast brushed against his arm. But most of the time he was enchanted with having one girl, and felt free of the tensions of having to pursue many different ones. All in all, he liked being married.

Things between him and Etta-Sue were even better now, for they no longer had to sneak or pretend. Missus Scott gave them a new double bed and another room on the third floor, which Etta-Sue fixed as a nice living room where they entertained their few friends, usually Hardie and whatever girl he might be cultivating.

They ate meals with Missus Scott and now both women pampered him.

"You want more meat, honey?" Etta-Sue put several spoon-fuls of stew onto his plate before he could say he was no longer hungry.

"Maybe he want some more rice too." Missus Scott was on his left, Etta-Sue across from him.

"No thanks, Missus Scott. I'm full."

"You supposed to call me Mama, remember? Nonsense, boy, you need more food than you been eating."

"Let me cut your meat, honey."

He was about to say it would not be necessary, but Etta-Sue had already snatched away his knife and fork.

He crammed down the helping, and before they could offer more, stood up. "I got to go to work." He started toward the door.

Etta-Sue followed, speaking back into the kitchen. "I'll be down in a minute, Mama." There was a sly smile in her voice. "Now, I got to say good-bye to my husband." She came to his side, took his elbow and guided him down the hall. "Here the steps."

"I know that, Etta-Sue."

"Of course you do." She continued to guide him.

On the third floor they entered their bedroom. "Hey, Etta-Sue, why don't you come by tonight? We got a new drummer, pretty good. Not that same heavy-handed old man."

She had released him at the door. He had gone to the bed, where now he sat running his fingers over his instrument. The night before a key had begun to stick and he had been attempt-ing to repair it himself. He still might have to take it to the repair shop. "What you say?" She had not answered.

She came from the doorsill to the bed, sat beside him, put her arm around him, and kissed his forehead. "I really tired, honey."

All at once, she sounded it. "But I hope it really good for you."
She kissed his cheek. "I be waiting for you."

He was disappointed. He had very much wanted her to come
tonight. Recently his own playing had improved greatly, probably because things had been going well for him with her. He
forced himself to smile, turned to her and kissed her lips hard.
He liked the way she kissed. "That's all right, Etta-Sue."

But he had not really responded to what she had last said and
a note of unhappiness was in her voice now. "You ain't mad, is
you?"

"Naw. I know you work hard." He sighed and got up. "Well,
got to get over there." He went to the closet for his coat, returned to the bed. "You be waiting up for me?"

This made her happier. "That what I said, honey."

He bent to her voice, found her mouth with his lips. "You be
all set to go—hear?"

"Oh, Ludlow." She was embarrassed. He wondered why she
was sometimes more embarrassed now than she had been before
they were married. He remembered how she had joked that day
about losing her underpants.

He told her good-bye and went downstairs. Missus Scott
was waiting for him near the front door. "I see some clouds up
there, boy. You best carry your coat."

"I just has to get wet then, ma'am. Ain't got no time now."
He opened the door quickly and was in the street.

It was a week night, but it was spring too and people had
come out onto their porches to talk and take the breezes from the
Gulf of Mexico. He caught snatches of conversation as he passed,
tapping his cane rapidly; he was anxious to play tonight.

Hardie came with a girl, telling Ludlow as they were heading
for the stage that he had met her in front of the barbershop.

"I just standing out there, watching asses, you know. So here she comes, looking like she trying to beat out six-eight with her butt. So I step up and say, 'Excuse me, miss, I'm a visiting preacher and I wonder if you can kindly tell me how to get to the Our Lord the Holy Savior Church?'"

"How you planning to explain working here?" Ludlow set his case on the piano and snapped it open.

"You ain't let me finish, man. So she looks me over and I'm thinking it a good thing I got on my black suit. Maybe she go for my stuff. But that ain't the way it is. She looks at me some more and then she snorts, and says, 'Why you no-good lie-telling fool! Here you standing in front of a God damn barbershop inspecting my cheeks and you asking me to believe you a visiting preacher.' So I starts thinking I can't hit a home run every time. But then I look up and she starting to chuckle and then she laughing and then she howling and she don't stop for ten minutes, all the time saying, 'A visiting preacher! He say he a visiting preacher!' Finally she stops and looks at me kinda serious, like she planning to rub my ass raw cursing at me. 'Come on now,' she say, 'what you really do?' I say I'm a musician. And she changes again. I mean, she look like I told her I was the President and she'd believed me. I mean, she was impressed out her clothes—or leastways I hope so."

Ludlow played a few warm-up notes. "So it come out all right."

"No, man! You ain't got the point. Sure it come out right, but she the first girl I ever met in my entire life who was impressed with the truth!" He paused. "She went for the God damn truth, man!"

After the set, Ludlow joined Hardie and the girl at a table. Her voice was shrill and hard to endure, but Ludlow liked her immediately. "So this the visiting preacher's friend, huh? You a altar boy?"

"That right, baby." He was smiling. "I give the sacraments."

"But only to his wife," Hardie added.

"He married, Hardie? You married, Ludlow?"

"Five months, about." He was surprised at the pride in his voice.

"You don't look old enough to be quite weaned yet." She was astonished.

"I ain't." He puckered his lips.

Hardie roared immediately, getting the joke, and in a moment so did the girl. Then she stopped. "You weaned yet, Hardie?"

"Not on your life—even if I ain't drunk milk in years."

They all laughed. Ludlow laughed until his temples ached.

At the end of the evening they stood outside Boone's and said their good-byes. If he knew Hardie, Ludlow would never meet the girl again.

"You going the other way, right?" Ludlow was always a bit sad when Boone's closed.

"Yeah." Hardie patted Ludlow's arm, then turned toward the girl. "We going to your place, right, baby?"

"We going." Liquor and loud talking had made her hoarse. "But first I want some breakfast, some ham and eggs and grits."

"Awh, baby, let's go home." There was a whine in Hardie's voice. Ludlow smiled.

The girl stomped her heels, her voice angry. "Take it easy, man. I'm planning to give up some. But we got all day for that. Right now I'm hungry."

Hardie laughed. "Okay, baby, you the boss. Lead on." He poked Ludlow in the ribs. They started away, the girl's heels cracking unevenly on the pavement, echoing against the faces of the buildings. Ludlow smiled, enjoying the racket and the good, deep tingle it gave him. He shook his head, remembering the old days when he would have been following that sound. He started home.

The memories of a good evening of playing and talking were still with him when he arrived home, crept up the stairs, and opened the door to their room.

"Ludlow?" Etta-Sue did not speak as if she had been sleeping; there was no fuzziness in her voice.

"You been up all night?"

She hesitated. "Yes. You could tell from my voice?"

"Sure." He sat down on the edge of the bed and ran his fingers over her face, pausing at her eyes, which seemed to be squinting, then down to her breasts, a bit cold, and over her warm stomach. She was wearing a cotton nightgown. She should have been naked. "Even with this thing on, you feel good. Let me get myself in there with you."

She was silent while he undressed and got into bed. He slid a strap off her shoulder and ran his palm lightly across the nipple of her breast. "How you been, Etta-Sue?" He put his arms around her and found her as rigid, as tense as she had been that first time. "What's the matter?" He was hurt that she was not responding.

"Ludlow, you happy?" She was quite troubled.

He was bewildered now. "Sure, Etta-Sue."

"Ludlow, I'm making a baby."

He hoped the lights were out. He did not know what look had crossed his face, but whatever, he wanted it hidden. He realized he had to say something, anything. "No fooling?"

"No fooling. I ain't had—well, you know. I remembered because last time was the weekend of Mama's church supper. And now it almost ten weeks from then. That why I didn't want to come tonight. I got dizzy coming up the stairs." This had come out in a stream, with few breaths taken.

He still worried about the light. He had to find out if the room was dark. He reached up and touched her eyes. "The light in your eyes, Etta-Sue?" Any answer at all would do.

"No, it out. You happy about it?"

She was asking about the baby. "Yeah. Hey, that great news." He said this not because he believed it, or even did not believe it, but because he knew it was the only thing to say. He did not yet know what he believed.

She hugged him. "I'm so glad you feel that way. I really want a baby."

He pushed his face into the pillow so that if light was coming from the street, or if day was breaking, she would not be able to see his expression. Anxiously he chased after his feelings. He was going to be a father, but he had never been within twenty feet of a baby. Some nights, while still in the Home, from the other side of the building, the crying of babies would carry to him. He would lie in his bed, surrounded by the deep breathing of the other boys, wondering what babies were like. He knew they grew up to be men and women, but not how much like men and women they already were. For Ludlow, a baby had never been more than a noise no less than twenty feet away. "When it happening? I mean—"

"I guess in seven months if I really am. I mean, I still might not be." For an instant he felt relieved, but tried to keep his body the same as it had been a moment before. She had not stopped talking. "But I pretty sure I am. I can feel the change." He realized then that he did not want her to have a baby. But having no reason to dislike babies, he wondered why he did not want her to have one.

"You sure you happy about it?" She seemed to doubt him.

He could have told the truth, could have said he was not sure, but it would not have helped anyone. She would be having a baby no matter how he felt. "Sure, Etta-Sue. That real great." He tried to sound enthusiastic, and he succeeded.

7

The seven months passed quickly. And now things were quite different. The two women paid little attention to him. Missus Scott fluttered and clucked only for Etta-Sue, and as her stomach grew large, Etta-Sue began paying more attention to it than to Ludlow, so much so that he began to think of her stomach and himself as rivals. He remained bewildered by the entire situation and was occasionally resentful. He felt himself a complete outsider to the excitement. Because Boone's was more his world now than anyplace else, he began to spend a great deal more time there, even some long afternoons, when, alone in the empty bar, he would pick out tunes on the piano or practice his own instrument.

Not long before the baby was born, standing at the bar one night, he was greeted by a familiar voice. "How Mister Lightning Rod doing?"

He had not made love to Etta-Sue in almost a month; the memories and guilt brought back by the voice made him want the body it had come from. He remembered too the promise he had made himself walking home from her house. He knew more than enough now to prove himself. "How you been, Malveen?"

She did not answer the question. "Small-Change say you married."

He nodded. It was a little hard to believe he was married now.

She hesitated. "I seen her on the street, I think. When's the blessed event?" She was trying to be sarcastic, but in her voice was an uneasiness she could not hide. He realized for the first time that she might be as much as ten years older than Etta-Sue.

"Not long now." He sipped from the drink in front of him. "What you doing here? I thought you said you wouldn't work outa here no more."

"I ain't working tonight."

His glass was sweating, cold. "Must be doing okay, taking nights off."

She did not comment. He wondered if her body still felt the same. The softness might have become flabby. Whores aged quickly.

"Since you ain't working, I'll buy you a drink." Even as he spoke he realized there was a quality in his voice he had not planned.

She paused before she answered. "So, little Mister Lightning Rod ain't had none lately, huh? Why, little boy, I can read it in your face. And you want old Malveen to give you some tonight."

He realized she must have seen hundreds of men like him, all of them waiting impatiently until the women they had married finished having babies and became wives again. "That's it, Malveen." He admitted it.

"Okay, little boy, you're on. I'll wait for you." She walked away.

At five they went to her house. They did not speak or touch one another. After a year and a half, he remembered the way almost perfectly. In her room, still without speaking, she closed and locked the door, kicked off her shoes, and unzipped her dress. "Everybody for hisself." She finished undoing her snaps, sliding out of her underclothes.

He undressed and they got into bed. She was too soft; he did not like the feel of her. But he was good to her and felt pride as she moaned and murmured. He made certain she had finished before he turned himself loose.

A minute later, she began pushing him. Tired, but relieved, he rolled off her. "Okay, baby?" He wanted her to say it had been good.

"Leave the five on the table, man."

He did not understand her. This was what she had wanted, had expected so long before. But he nodded, sat up, found his pants and wallet, and pulled out the bill. It had been worth five dollars. He felt turned inside out. He got up and started to dress.

She spoke to him from the bed. "Oh, it was good all right, little boy, but you owed me for one, remember?" Then her voice changed. "Next time's free."

He knotted his tie. "Won't be no next time, Malveen."

In fifteen minutes he was home, in bed, beside the sleeping Etta-Sue. She was on her side facing him. He lay on his back and with his right hand stroked her stomach. It was not the touch of pride or affection, but of inquiry, as if, through the skin and muscle, he could somehow feel the baby, and once and for all know what it was, and what he felt for it. Once it moved, and he drew his hand away. Soon, he was thinking, it would be born and he would have Etta-Sue back again. When the baby was born things would be the way they had once been and he would not have to visit any more Malveens. Then it would be good between him and Etta-Sue. It would not be long now.

8

Etta-Sue had a girl. She and Missus Scott had a girl's name picked: Bertha, after Missus Scott. But the woman who typed out the certificate made a mistake and the name appeared Bethrah. Etta-Sue and Missus Scott tried to have the mistake corrected, but none of the officials they talked to were sufficiently interested in the name of one Negro baby to do anything. Bethrah was the baby's legal name.

Because of the baby, Etta-Sue informed Ludlow, he would have to practice at Boone's. He would go there in the early afternoon, soon after his breakfast, and stay until five in the morning. The early morning hours were the only ones he was near Etta-Sue. But the baby's crib was in the corner of their room, and even if they were making love, when the baby cried, Etta-Sue would interrupt them and jump out of bed. He soon began to realize that his days alone with Etta-Sue would never return.

Still, he tried; he hoped. He did not go back to Malveen's

116

bed nor did he go with any of the girls who nightly invited him, with a certain tone in their voices if not openly, to their rooms. But he was bewildered too, did not know how to fit into this new life and believed guiltily that he was at fault.

When it first came home, he made an effort to know the baby, would ask to hold in his arms the small, screeching voice, but Etta-Sue would not permit it. "You might trip over something and drop her. I'd worry myself to death about her." After a while he no longer tried to know the baby. After all, it was Etta-Sue's baby. She had always wanted it; he had never wanted it enough. For him the baby remained a small cry in the corner of the room.

And still he hoped and tried. Two months after the baby was born he became eighteen. He did not leave Rodney's band as he had planned, because he could not get a definite commitment from any café in New Marsails. He did not want to risk being out of work. Some of the owners said they would have to hear any new group before they could hire it. Others had heard that Ludlow would sometimes experiment; they were not sure their customers would like Ludlow's playing without Rodney's firm guiding hand. Finally he talked Rodney into raising his salary to the level of the rest of the musicians', hoping that if he brought home more money it would impress Etta-Sue. But at the time that he was telling her about his raise she was holding the crying baby, and did not pay much attention to him.

He wished there was someone he could ask about it, someone who could give him just a few clues about how to handle the situation, but there was no one. Hardie was not married—was, in fact, opposed to the very idea of it—and could not help. Ludlow knew no one else. Finally he shrugged away the idea. Besides, he did not like to ask for help because whoever he asked would have an advantage over him. He decided he would wait; perhaps something would happen, perhaps Etta-Sue would become less enthralled with being a mother. And anyway, waiting was the only thing he could do.

Ludlow sat on the stage in the empty café, trying to play something difficult, something he had learned from an early Norman Spencer recording. It was late spring now, steaming weather in New Marsails, but all of the café's windows were nailed shut. He believed that if only he could get a lungful of good air, he could play correctly.

At first he thought a cat was scratching at the screen door and he ignored it. He did not like cats. But when the scratching became a knocking, he realized someone wanted to get in. He picked up his cane, came down off the stage, and traveled the length of the room, his fingers on the bar. He waited for the knocking again and when it came, directed himself toward it, knowing there was nothing between the end of the bar and the door. He spoke through the screening. "Yeah?"

"This Boone's Café, ain't it?" It was a boy's voice, perhaps about fourteen years old. He recognized something in it, but could not immediately place it. Then he knew; it was very like the voice of his master in the Home, a voice coming through a mouthful of water.

"Right. What you want?" The slight warm breeze felt good against his face.

The boy hesitated, probably studying Ludlow's eyes. "Got a telegram here. From New York." The boy continued to stare; it was in his voice. "For Mister Ledlow Washington?" The boy read the name.

"Ledlow?"

"That right. Washington."

Ludlow opened the screen door. "I guess that's me." He extended his hand.

"You Ledlow Washington?"

"It Ludlow, but it me anyway. Give it here." He was excited; he had never before received a telegram.

"But you ain't Ledlow Washington."

"Go on, boy. They made a mistake, is all."

The boy was silent for a moment. Finally: "Okay. Here." He put the telegram into Ludlow's hand. "Hey, you a musician?" The boy must have been listening to Ludlow practice. Ludlow turned back into the café; the boy followed.

"Yeah."

"I play clarinet in the high school band. One day I'm getting me a tenor." He was proud of that.

"How much I owe you?"

The boy ignored him. "I'll play that tenor so good I'll have my own band and wear a white suit, up in front, and the girls'll love me."

"What's the bill, boy?"

"What? Oh, nothing. Already paid." The boy was unhappy to be dragged away from his dreams.

Ludlow fished into his pocket, found a quarter and gave it to the boy.

"That what I'm planning to do. I'm going—"

"You read?" There was no one in the café and Ludlow could not wait to discover what the telegram said.

"Who, me? Yeah. I in high school, I told you."

"Read this to me." He extended the telegram, felt it being taken out of his hand. There was the crackle of tearing paper.

"It say: *To Mister Ledlow Washington, Boone's Café, New*

Marsails. Are you eighteen yet if . . . yes, I mean, *if yes come New York can still use you will pay . . . fare,* oh it means here, *will pay fare hundred a week reply Inez Cunningham.*" The return address was a well-known New York theater. "A hundred dollars a week? Holy catfish!"

Ludlow's stomach had gone flat. She had remembered him and wanted him in New York. He had the boy read the telegram once again. When the boy had finished, Ludlow had memorized it.

"Hey, that Inez Cunningham? I mean, Inez Cunningham?"

Ludlow had already started toward the stage for his coat. He had to tell Etta-Sue. This would change everything between them. They would go to New York, the baby too. They were all going to New York.

The boy had followed him. "That really the singer Inez Cunningham?"

"No one but."

"You going to New York to play with her?" The boy touched his elbow.

"If I got to walk all the way on my hands." Even if she were not paying his fare he would be going.

"I'll see you, Mister Washington." The boy turned, started to run. "I'm going home to practice!" And he was gone, slamming the door.

Ludlow paid no attention. He was already in his coat. He closed up his instrument case, leaving it on the piano.

He tapped his way home, trying as he went to imagine New York. Musicians had come through New Marsails talking about it, but they could only give him an idea of it. They had told him about the sights, but that did not tell him anything. He had asked about the sounds, the smells, the taste of the air, but they could never tell him such things. He would have to find out for himself.

Etta-Sue and Missus Scott were in the kitchen. "What you doing here? It only four-thirty." Etta-Sue was sitting at the table.

"Hello, Lud—" Missus Scott stopped; she must have noticed his face. "What's wrong, boy?"

"I got me a job, a good one!" He stood just inside the kitchen door, shouting.

"Shhh! The baby's sleeping in Mama's room. That good news, Ludlow." Etta-Sue did not sound as if she had looked up at him yet.

"I'm proud of you, boy." Missus Scott was more interested.

"With Inez Cunningham." He said no more, certain the name would impress them.

"Oh? She coming to town?" Etta-Sue was facing up now.

"No. We going to New York! She sent me a telegram. She paying my fare and—one hundred United States dollars a week!"

The room was silent. They were not cooking dinner yet. They had even seemed to stop breathing.

"Here's the telegram." He pulled the envelope from his pocket, came into the room and put it on the table.

Etta-Sue's chair squeaked; there was the rustle of paper. He waited for her laughter or tears or for her to lunge into his arms. It would feel good to have her in his arms at this moment.

The telegram rustled again. "Read it, Mama." Missus Scott's footsteps stomped across the floor; the paper crackled, and a moment later, a third time, sliding into its envelope.

"What you planning to answer, Ludlow?"

He did not understand. They were going to New York. But something was wrong because she did not understand that. "Etta-Sue, we—"

"Ludlow, this my home. I'm happy here. I thought you was too."

"Well, sure I am, Etta-Sue. But we got a chance to go with Inez Cunningham—me, you and the baby too. We going to New York." He would not have believed that she would want to do anything else. For a moment he could not hold a thought in his head. Sounds whined and popped, her voice as it was at this moment, as it had been when she said "Oh, Ludlow" the first time they made love. In his mind, she joked about not being able to find her underpants, she told him not to give up music, to wait just one short year. Then all the sounds stopped. There was only his heart beating, and his breathing, and, far away, cars in the street. "You mean you don't want me to go? You want me to turn her down? Jesus!" He stretched the name.

"You got a good job here. And in a while you'll have your own band. What you want to go chasing to New York for?" She was nervous now.

"You really don't want me to take the job. Jesus Christ!" He spoke softly, more to himself than to her.

"No. Don't you like the life we got here?"

He shook his head, thinking about what Hardie had said to him almost fifteen months before, about making certain the girl he married was really with him. He had made such a huge mistake, had been so far off the point that it was almost funny. "I ain't got no more life here, Etta-Sue."

"Why you say that, Ludlow?" Etta-Sue and Missus Scott spoke almost in unison.

He shook his head again, and, unable to keep a smile from creeping across his face, turned toward the door. There was just one more thing he had to find out.

122

"Ludlow? Where you going?" Etta-Sue jumped from the table, banging her chair. "Mama, he look crazy. He smiling."

He was already heading down the hall, counting his steps. After seven he stopped.

"Mama!" Etta-Sue was screaming from the kitchen door. "Mama! He going in to the baby!"

He entered Missus Scott's room, advanced to the bed, where he knew the baby would be sleeping, surrounded by pillows. He was no longer smiling.

Etta-Sue was at the door. "Ludlow! Don't touch her." There was a deep panic rasping in her throat. "Ludlow!" She took two steps into the room.

He turned around, speaking to her calmly. "Etta-Sue, if you come near me, I'll throw this baby out the window."

She stopped, then turned and ran from the room, back down the hall. "Mama, he planning to kill her. He say—" she did not finish. The two women came to the door.

He spoke over his shoulder now. "If you two come in this room, I'll wring its neck like a chicken." Behind him they were whispering.

He had already located the bundled blanket. Now he undid it and could feel the tiny bones, the soft skin, the toes, the nails no bigger than the heads of pins. He ran his hand up the legs, up to the diaper, damp and knotted. He smelled the powder and oil Etta-Sue had rubbed on the small body. Its stomach heaved up and down. Its chest was not even as wide as his hand. His fingers felt its heart thumping like a dull clock through skin as thin as cloth. The head was covered with soft hair. He wondered what color it was—probably red like Etta-Sue's. There was a nose smaller even than a key on an alto saxophone and two eye sockets and ears. His daughter—but he would not have known that if

123

he had not been told. He closed the blankets, straightened up, and spoke toward the whispering women. "Okay, ladies, don't worry yourselves. It all yours now." He walked toward the door, nodding his head. "I'm going to New York."

They did not answer. He pushed by them, his elbow brushing Etta-Sue's breast. They were filled with fluid now and each time he had tried to touch them, she had complained he was hurting her. Behind him the women rushed into the room and slammed the door.

It did not take long to pack. He would need his two suits and some shirts, underwear, and socks. He would have to tell Rodney and pick up his instrument at Boone's. He left the Braille music books and everything else. With one hundred dollars a week he could buy anything he wanted in New York. He did not leave Etta-Sue any money. She had a baby and perhaps that was all she had ever wanted.

Etta-Sue and Missus Scott were waiting at the foot of the steps when he came down, but they said nothing as he tapped past them and into the street.

PART FOUR

INTERVIEW . . .

What's all this mess about me coming to New York and inventing modern jazz? Right out, there two things wrong with that.

First of all, I don't think I invented it alone. I mean, lots of us did it. We all sat up in Harlem and put the new stuff together. It wasn't just me. I got things from them; they got things from me.

And second of all, if I did invent it, like they say, I invented it back in New Marsails in Bud Rodney's band, or maybe even before that, in the blind home. Because all my life I been playing what I liked. Take Norman Spencer. He coulda been the one who invented it hisself. He was doing new things way back in the twenties. I only listened and played what I liked in him and that was that. I didn't decide one day—blam!—I'd play something new, because I been playing pretty much the same since I was thirteen, except now maybe I can play a little faster. But that ain't genius. That's just practicing.

I

He sat up on the hard seat, his back aching, his legs cramped, his feet asleep. A moment before, the rattling rumble of the train had deepened and he knew it was almost in the station. He fingered his instrument case, amazed, as he was from time to time, that the ability to produce noises from a twisted metal tube encrusted with smooth buttons could actually bring him this far. He had just left Inez Cunningham.

He had stayed with her for three years. That was enough. After the excitement of New York, of one hundred dollars a week, of one thousand people in an audience, after the excitement of all this had faded, he had been surprised to discover he was not satisfied. He did not think he was getting enough opportunity to play and improve. In the back of his mind he still dreamed of having his own group, perhaps even a big band. Although in the beginning he had learned a great deal from Inez, he thought now he had learned all she could teach him. But still he had not left her immediately; that would have been foolish.

He waited, and finally he was told that Jack O'Gee, leader of one of the two or three good bands in the country, had said he wished there was someone like Ludlow Washington in his orchestra. Ludlow sent O'Gee a telegram asking if he would equal the salary Inez was giving him. O'Gee, answering the same day, said he would, and told Ludlow to join the band in Chicago.

Somewhere west of Buffalo, just as the train broke from a roaring tunnel, he had begun to wonder whether it had been a smart thing to leave Inez. After all, he had never expected more than a living from music and Inez had given him that. Besides, she offered security; she would be popular and working for the next twenty years. Bands were another thing. Sometimes there was a great deal of work and then, a year later, night clubs and dance halls would be hiring nothing but small groups. He wondered why he had not thought of all this before, realizing vaguely that in the last three years his entire attitude toward music had changed.

He had been to Chicago several times in the past three years and so without difficulty made the trip from the station to the Southside hotel where the O'Gee orchestra was staying.

His room, like a hundred others he had lived in, was three paces wide and four long, a bed taking most of the room, with a dresser, and a chair in one corner. There were towels on the arm of the chair.

A bellboy, reeking of sweat and hair pomade, had carried his bag to the room. Ludlow's fingers were already on the small locks when there was a knock at the door.

"Hello, man. Welcome to Chicago."

Ludlow swung the door wide and stepped out of the way, smiling. "What you doing in Chicago, Hardie?"

"I been with O'Gee four months. I made it, man. How about

me!" Hardie's excited voice crossed the room. "And now you here too."

Ludlow nodded. "How far'm I from the chair?"

"Further left. You look older, man. I guess it the clothes; you don't dress like no farm boy no more."

"Don't kid me. I look older because I'm tired as hell. I been playing with Inez from nine to three, and been jamming from three to seven or eight. But man, you should hear the stuff."

"I did." Hardie was sitting on the bed. "On one of the records you made with Inez. You played a pretty eight bars. You two was so sweet together! I don't understand how you coulda left her. You two sounded like lovers." Hardie's voice turned sly. "Say, you weren't doing the dirty thing, was you?"

Ludlow smiled. "No, man, nothing like that." If anything, Inez had mothered him, but mostly, if they were not practicing or performing, they did not even meet. Their relationship was built only around music. "I left because of them God damn little eight-bar solos. They wasn't enough. To play something good, or hear it, you got to have eight choruses. That's why I quit her. She'd sing, then here I come with my eight bars. I just get an idea going and she back again. That's why I had to quit and come to O'Gee."

Hardie was timid. "Them eight bars was pretty anyways. . . . Remember that time back with Rodney when we played that old ballad and you did them things to it and Rodney bawled you out? Them eight bars was just like that."

Ludlow had completely forgotten that other time. He had always thought that he had improved to where he was now.

Hardie continued: "All the guys in the band really excited about you coming. Some can even play your solos note for note.

I can do that." He was quite proud. "Some guys even writing them down to find out what chords you making."

"They really do that?"

"Sure, man. I heard guys say you doing things ain't never been done before, guys who seen you in sessions with Norman Spencer."

What Hardie said silenced them both. Ludlow was embarrassed and did not know what to reply. He had realized his playing was different, but he had thought that was simply because he was better than most. He had known too that he was tired of what music sounded like—heavy and loud—and so at sessions he had suggested to the other men how they might play a certain song. But he had never thought of this as a new style; he was simply trying to get a sound to the music that he liked.

Finally Ludlow could no longer endure the silence and flung out a question. "Well, how Rodney when you left?" He got up and walked to the bed, began to unpack.

Hardie moved to the chair. "Same old stuff. I was getting tired myself, but I never thought I'd get a better thing, until O'Gee come down to play a dance and heard me and asked me to take his second chair." He paused, cleared his throat. "Etta-Sue come in a couple times. . . ."

Ludlow realized Hardie had brought this up because he felt it his duty. If Ludlow did not want to talk about Etta-Sue, he did not have to pick up the thread. "What'd she want?" He tried to make his voice cold. He had found his handkerchiefs.

"Wanted to know where you was."

His heart was beating wildly. He had been away from New Marsails three years now, but from time to time he still thought of Etta-Sue. He did not want to go back to her or want her to come to him. But, lying alone some nights, he remembered strange things, not just the steady love-making. It had not been at all steady after she became pregnant. He remembered, rather, things like walking home from Boone's in the rain, undressing and crawling into bed beside her, feeling her throbbing with heat.

Hardie continued, "She didn't say nothing. I mean, about—you know what I mean. . . . I even seen the kid a couple times."

Ludlow opened a dresser drawer and dropped in his five shirts. "What she look like?"

"Well, you know, she a baby. Got this dark red hair, not light like Etta-Sue's, but—she look like you. She light like her mama, but she look like you, and I'd say she planning to be big as a fire engine." Hardie, in telling this, had enough enthusiasm for the both of them. "Well, anyway, I seen Etta-Sue just before I left and she say—I don't like telling you this, man—she say she going to Alabama for a divorce."

Ludlow's stomach growled. "You know a place we can get some good down-home food?"

"Sure." Hardie was sad. "Hey, Ludlow, I'm sorry."

"Then after while we'll come back and you can play me the book."

"Yeah, sure." Suddenly Hardie had shaken his mood. "But I want you to meet someone first."

In the lobby Hardie stopped, told Ludlow to wait, and went off to the desk. He was back in a moment. "Okay. We'll get that food in a second." He was nervous, probably having seen Ludlow shift impatiently from one foot to the other.

High heels, a loosely swinging step, came across the marble floor and stopped near them. Hardie squeezed his elbow. "Baby, this the great Ludlow Washington." Hardie's voice was closer now. "Ludlow, this my wife, Juanita."

132

"Jesus, Hardie, what you go and do that for?" He smiled. "Hello, Juanita. He ain't giving you too much trouble, is he?"

"Should say so." Her voice was reedy. He had never liked lisps, but liked hers, which flooded her S's. She was a little taller than Hardie.

"Sounds all right. Where you find her?"

"Right here, first night on the job." It meant a great deal to Hardie that Ludlow should approve of her. "We been married three months."

"I hope you get all the luck I didn't."

Hardie coughed, obviously moved. "Let's get you fed."

They went into the street, passing the smell of chicken and ribs which came from open stores, passing mock arguments and whooping laughter, passing groups of children chanting songs to the smack of a rope on pavement. Finally Hardie led him into a small store smelling of grease, dust, and good food. There was a jukebox and Inez was singing.

They slid into a booth, ordered food and beer. Ludlow's fingers searched a scar in the wooden seat. He listened to his own solo, attempting in vain to find this new style of music Hardie had been talking about.

"You wrung that song dry!" There was the pop of a kiss. "She likes your playing too, don't you, baby."

"Hardie says you married too, and got a baby."

Hardie sighed, but said nothing.

"I ain't married no more, sweetie. But don't feel bad about it."

"Why'd you break up?"

Hardie sighed again. "Baby, don't—"

"It all right, Hardie. I don't know, sweetie. I think it was I wanted to go to New York and she didn't."

"And she didn't end up coming with you?"

Hardie was getting angry. "Juanita, for Christ's sake, let him—"

"Hold it, man. No, sweetie, she didn't want to leave down home."

"Stupid!" Under the table, her heel clicked once, sharp and hard.

"New York ain't all that much." Women always wanted to go to New York.

"I ain't talking about New York." She leaned across the table. "What I mean is, you may want your husband not to go, and may try to talk him out of going, but when the chips go down, you pack your hot comb and you go with him. That's all. You don't never let no man wander off nowheres by himself."

Ludlow held back a smile. "What if he want to go to Alaska and play for the Eskimos?"

"Then you pack your hot comb and your woollies and you tag right along." She was serious.

Ludlow took out a cigarette, put it into his mouth, struck a match and, feeling the heat on his face, drew smoke into his lungs. "Hardie? You don't never got to look behind you to know who's there."

"Yeah." He was still angry about Juanita's lack of tact.

The beer came, and Hardie said he wanted to make a toast. "Here's hoping you get something nice for yourself, Ludlow."

Ludlow nodded, raised his glass; the beer, cold and bitter, started down, expanding. "I'll drink to that, man."

2

Ludlow had known Norman Spencer for seven years
now, through his three years with Inez and the following four
with Jack O'Gee. He had met the old pianist within a week of his
first arrival in New York. Inez Cunningham, although she had
told Ludlow she would probably regret it, had introduced them.
Spencer was very small for a grown man; his voice started just
at Ludlow's chest, was high, breathy, and surprisingly Northern-
sounding for a man who had been born and raised in the South.
Spencer did not talk at all about himself, and, even after seven
years, Ludlow had never found out where the pianist lived,
whether or not he was married, had any children, or even what he
did until he came to work at eight o'clock. The four things Ludlow did know about Spencer were that he smoked cigars, was
thirty years older than Ludlow, that he had come from the South,
and that he refused to leave Harlem.

Ludlow was never sure that he and Spencer were friends,
though he knew the pianist respected his musicianship. Ludlow

finally decided he was Norman Spencer's pupil. Thinking back to what his master in the Home had told him—that everyone had a master until he died—Ludlow decided that if he could choose his master, it would certainly be Norman Spencer.

Whenever he was in New York, Ludlow would end the evening at the bar where Spencer worked, listening to, and most times playing with, the pianist. Each time they played together Ludlow found something new in the pianist's music, something which gave him enough ideas to last a month. Ludlow did not copy Norman Spencer. It was rather that the pianist made him think.

They had just finished a number, and while the audience, composed mostly of musicians, applauded, Ludlow rested his elbow on top of the upright piano and asked Spencer what he wanted to play next.

"A cigar." The piano top slammed down. Spencer came around to Ludlow's side and took his elbow.

They left the low stage and sat at a table. In a moment a waitress stood beside them. Ludlow ordered drinks, his nostrils already taking in gusts of the pianist's cigar smoke. Before meeting Spencer, Ludlow had always associated cigars with the Warden. But he had outgrown that, and now, even smoked them himself.

"Mister Spencer, I want to ask you something."

"About what?"

"About you." He usually did not ask the pianist questions; rather he would make a statement and hope the older man would comment.

Spencer puffed his cigar. The cash register belled and slid open.

Ludlow had been on tour with O'Gee the past three months. He had been thinking about his question all during the trip.

"Listen, Mister Spencer, I been playing since I was sixteen, and up until now I always thought I was playing for money. Now I think maybe I ain't been playing for money at all. But if I ain't doing it for money, then why the hell am I doing it?" He stopped. "What I want to know is, why are you playing music, Mister Spencer?"

The pianist sucked on his cigar ten or more times. Then he scratched the stubble of his face. "Don't know nothing else."

Ludlow was familiar with that answer. "I used to say that too, Mister Spencer." The waitress returned with their drinks. "But that ain't enough. I mean, we could learn something else, even you, old as you are, even me, blind and all." He was getting excited.

The pianist was quiet for a long while and just when Ludlow was convinced he had refused to talk, he started: "Some folks around think we artists, like classical musicians. Maybe we are."

Ludlow did not understand the connection. His dismay must have crossed his face.

"Ludlow, there only two reasons why people do things—because they want to and because they got to. The only time you can do something good is when you want to. Now maybe sometimes you can want to do something so bad that after a while it's like you got to. But now instead of being made to do it by someone else, you making yourself do it, and then maybe you an artist. Okay, now take you. You could be playing like everybody else and then instead of being in O'Gee's band, he'd be in yours. For some reason you don't play like no one else. But ain't nobody forcing you to be different. So maybe you better forget about money because if you really cared about it, you'd be playing the way that makes the most money."

Ludlow was more confused than ever. "Then why do I play?"

"Hell, boy, I don't know. Ask your mama!"

They sat silently for a few moments, until Ludlow was torn from his thoughts by a high-pitched laugh. Spencer gave his arm a hard poke. "White folks! Shit!"

"White folks?" No white person had ever entered this place in the seven years Ludlow had been coming here.

"Bringing their frantic selves uptown."

"What they doing?"

"Looking around, is all, waiting for something to happen." The pianist mimicked a white person: "Oh, niggers are so exciting, always raping and killing each other!"

Ludlow could not hold back a short laugh. "How many are they?"

"Three couples. Three pasty-faced men and three high-class chippies with their titties hanging out." He turned back to Ludlow. "You know, I ain't been out of Harlem in fifteen years. What for I want to go downtown and watch them dying in the streets. I'll stay up here where people ain't kidding themselves. They pushed us all together up here, but they still won't leave us alone. They got the idea they missing something, so they dress up and come here to see. I don't show them nothing." One of the white women was still laughing shrilly; she was drunk. "Oh, here come old pasty-faced Charlie now."

The table jumped. "Are you . . . Ludlow Washington?" The man was drunk too, trying very hard not to sound it.

"Sure. What you want?" Ludlow tilted his head up toward the man's voice.

"I've seen you . . . playing . . . lots of times. With Inez Cunningham. And with Jack O'Gee too and . . . with Inez Cunningham. Did I already say that?" He giggled. "Anyway . . . we're having a party later on tonight . . . and we'd like to you—

you to come if you want to. You don't have to play if you don't want to . . . but you can if you want to. Do you want to? . . . come?" The man gave him an address downtown. Ludlow had him repeat it, memorizing it, though he was not certain he would actually go.

"This is Norman Spencer. You heard of him?"

"Sure! Sure—God! . . . I heard of him. God! It's a pleasure to meet you, Mister Spencer. I have every one of your records, every one, even the ones on cylinders. I have them even."

Norman Spencer did not use his own voice. "You got all my records, boss? You do me an honor. Thank you, boss. Thank you very much—boss."

"God, Mister Spencer, I should thank you for making them." He was sincere. Ludlow felt a touch sorry for him.

"Oh, no, boss. Poor old colored jazz music player like me shouldn't never get thanked by no white man, boss. You the boss, boss."

Ludlow cut in. "You want Mister Spencer to come too?"

"Yes, if he would. We have a grand piano."

"A grand piano, boss? Really, a grand piano? I ain't never played on them. Only played a whorehouse upright piano in my life. Imagine old Norman T. Spencer on a real live grand piano—"

"All right, we'll be there." Too much blood had been drawn already.

"Yeah," Spencer grumbled.

"God, this is really wonderful. Thanks, Mister Washington. Thanks, Mister Spencer."

Ludlow nodded; beside him, the pianist still grumbled.

The man thanked them both again and left, crashing into the table nearest them.

Spencer filled the air and Ludlow's lungs with smoke. "We oughta round up twenty of the worst cutthroats we can find and loot that fancy address, chandeliers and all."

"He didn't seem too bad, Mister Spencer."

"White folks ain't never bad, Ludlow. They just weak. At least the ones we got here is weak. Here they round you up and push you in a slum, all the time telling you how much they love you. You take the Germans. Right now, they rounding up Jews and killing them. But they ain't spouting no shit about loving them. The white folks we got here ain't nearly that strong. You mark my words, don't never depend on no white man for nothing. He ain't strong enough to keep his promises." He beat the ash tray, grinding out his cigar.

"I'll remember that, Mister Spencer." Ludlow humored the pianist.

"Make sure you do." He stood up and sighed. "Let's play some." He grabbed Ludlow's elbow, almost pulling him to his feet, and they headed for the stage.

3

An hour later Ludlow started downtown. With him was Reno Tems, who played tenor with Norman Spencer, and whom Ludlow had met only a few nights before, when he returned to the city. He liked Reno's playing and hoped that if ever he formed his own group, he would be able to persuade Reno to join it.

At the end of this evening he had turned to Reno. "Your real name ain't Reno, is it?"

"No, sir. Edgar." He obviously did not like the name.

"Why they call you Reno?"

"I like to play cards a lot." Reno was at least a head taller than Ludlow, quite tall.

Ludlow laughed. "You ever get any white ass?"

Reno was puzzled. "Sir?"

"I got invited to a party, by them white folks over there?" He had decided to go now. He had never been inside of a fancy downtown place and did not want to miss the opportunity. "If you don't get some white ass, at least somebody may play cards with you."

He had sent Reno to get taxi fare from the man who had invited them, and then they had started out. Spencer had refused to join them on their expedition beyond the frontier of 110th Street.

Since it was not their money, Ludlow had the cab driver take them slowly through the park.

"This happen to you a lot?" Reno's voice was deep-throated and resonant; only by a certain timidity and enthusiasm did Ludlow guess Reno was young. It was obvious that he could not quite believe he was sitting in a taxi with Ludlow Washington on his way downtown to a white party.

"All the time." They passed the hollow clopping of horses' hoofs, the grating of steel-rimmed wheels on pavement. "No. This really the first time. But you get a lot of free drinks and free ass thrown at you."

"Man!" Reno threw himself into the seat.

"How old're you anyway?"

"Twenty." There was no great difference in their ages, but at twenty Ludlow had been with Inez Cunningham almost two years.

He knew Reno was from the South somewhere. "What you do before you come up here?" An ambulance rushed by, its siren curling in the quiet night.

"Went to school, college, taking music. But I wanted to play—you know, work."

"Why?" Ludlow was thinking about his conversation with Spencer. Perhaps Reno might give him a key to an idea of his own.

"Because it's the black man's music!" All at once the boy was

142

not at all timid. Ludlow smiled. "And we got to keep on working at it so everybody in the world'll know the black man created it."

Ludlow snorted. "I met some white boys who doing good things."

"They just copying us, that's all. We do all the creating. Like you."

Ludlow winced. "Listen, you do the playing and forget all this other stuff. When you up there trying to put something together, you ain't got time to think about all that mess!"

They left the park and soon the cab had stopped. Reno paid and helped Ludlow out and to the curb. The doorman who encountered them in the lobby asked them where they were going, and then called up. When he found out they were expected, he led them to the elevator and took them up, all the time mumbling to himself.

The party came through a heavy steel door to meet them—music, clicking glasses, people talking and laughing, several loud men, several shrill women.

Their host opened the door to them. "Hey, glad you came!"

Behind Ludlow the elevator door rattled shut; they had been watched just in case they did not belong.

"Didn't Mister Spencer come?" The host was disappointed.

"No, he never comes South," Ludlow deadpanned. Reno laughed.

"Well, hey, come on in. I'm really glad you came." He backed into the party. They followed him onto carpeting as thick as five bath towels. "Get these fellows a drink, will you?"

"Yes, sir. This way please." The girl's voice was a bit like Malveen's, though not nearly so Southern. With Reno guiding him, they zigzagged through the party, causing flickers of silence as they went. Ludlow knew they must be the only Negroes at the

143

party and that a good many people did not know how they came to be there.

He was between Reno and the girl. He was just about to ask her who she was and what she did there when her shoulder touched his. "You Ludlow Washington, ain't you?" Her whispering voice just carried over the jumble of shouts behind them.

He nodded, asked her about herself.

"Maid. I saw you uptown with Inez about six years ago. How'd they get you here?"

"Got invited. Your boss was uptown where I was playing." Ice tumbled into a glass. "Who this man anyways?"

"Can't answer now." She was a little nervous. "Would you come into the kitchen afterwhile?" A cold glass touched his hand, and she brushed by him.

He turned to Reno. "How's it look?"

"This place is fantastic. It's really beautiful." He paused. "I'm going to find the bathroom—okay?"

"Go on, man, you don't need permission."

He stood with his back to the table. Off to his right a record player was strutting old-time jazz. To the left, but several rooms away, someone was playing a piano.

"You're one of the musicians, aren't you?" a woman drawled at him. "We just loved your playing. I hope you'll play again tonight."

"Thanks." He nodded. He could not resist asking her the next question. "You from the South, ain't you?"

"Yes?" She was on her guard now. He could not understand why. She went on: "Now you listen to me for a moment. We're not all like that. Some of us are much better people for having come from the South. It was like being very ill and becoming

144

cured. We're a lot better than some Northerners who always say they're liberal. They've never been really tested."

At the beginning of her speech, Ludlow had been puzzled, but now he knew what kind of person, woman, she was. He knew already he did not want to talk to her, began plotting how to rid himself of her. "You know, I never did think of it like that before."

"Well, you certainly should have. Some of us are trying awfully hard." She did not sound too old, perhaps somewhere in her thirties.

He nodded sympathetically. "I'm sure you do, miss. In fact, I been coming around to the very selfsame conclusion myself. I mean, I'm beginning to realize some of the nicest white people I meet up here was born in the South. It a big thing for me to understand the South have nice people too. I had a lot to get over. I mean, it was the Klan blinded me."

She gasped. "Really? Oh, how terrible!"

"But I ain't nearly bitter as my friend. They killed his daddy and raped his mama and made him watch the whole thing." He had a difficult time trying not to laugh. "I think you oughta talk to him like you talked to me. It ain't good to be bitter like he is. It poisons your life."

"Yes, it certainly does." She was quite concerned for Reno. "Where is he?"

"But listen now, you better go and wait across the room until I talk to him, soften his heart a little. He so bitter and hates white people so bad he might call you out your name right here. He got to take me into the kitchen, but when he gets back, you just come over and talk to him. I mean, he really needs all your help."

"All right. You're sure he'll want to talk?"

"I'm sure. You know, a man really needs to tell his troubles to a woman. You could really help him, I'm sure. I mean, that's if you really interested in the Negro problem."

"Oh, I am, truly." She sucked her tongue several times. "Oh, he must be in such terrible anguish."

"He is, miss. But now you better get across the way before he come back. And, miss, thanks a lot."

"You're more than welcome." She left him waiting for Reno, who returned in another minute.

"You should see that bathroom, man! They got gold-rimmed toilet paper. They got two toilets and another thing that's about the size of a toilet, but looks more like a God damn bathtub! They got—"

"Listen, man, you want that white ass?"

"What?"

"Well, it up to you. There a white woman looking at us from across the room? She come about to my shoulder."

There was a pause. "I think so. But what—"

"Hold it. She from the South. And she trying singledhanded to make up for all the South's crimes. So I told her the Klan took my eyes out. Then I told her they killed your daddy and raped your mama and made you watch—"

"But my father's running a groc—"

"Wait, man. So I said for her to talk to you because you is one bitter nigger and need sympathy and help. She wants to prove all Southerners ain't bad. So if you like how she looks—you let her prove it! Understand now?"

"Sure, but—"

"Look, man, if you don't want to screw, maybe she'll play some God damn cards with you."

Reno laughed. "All right, Ludlow."

"So now take me into the kitchen."

Reno took his elbow and led him through a smooth-swinging door into a hallway, at the end of which was the kitchen. The air was much purer now, and smelled of cookies.

A newspaper rattled. "Hello, Mister Washington. Having a good time?" Actually, the maid's voice was much sweeter than Malveen's, and far more tired. It was really more like Etta-Sue's voice.

"All right." He remembered Reno. "This here is Reno. He'll be playing tenor in my new group."

"I will?" The boy was pleased and surprised.

"If you want. Find me a chair and go play some cards." Reno left him standing somewhere in the center of the large room, and scraped a chair across to him; Ludlow sat down. "Thanks. You put me in a taxi?" He was speaking to the maid.

"Sure." Her voice was smiling.

"Okay, Reno, go get your bitterness taken care of." Reno laughed as he started down the hall. Ludlow turned back to the maid and lit a cigarette. "You married?"

"Yes. And I have a little boy almost four." She was quite proud.

"Okay, now I don't got to do no lying. Don't feel like it to-night." He found himself thinking that his own child, the girl would be eight or nine years old soon. He wondered how it would be to have a child and be proud of it.

He sat quietly humming one of the chants the little girls of Harlem sang when they skipped rope.

Finally the newspaper rustled loudly to the floor. "Why'd you come, Mister Washington?"

"I wanted to find out how they live down here."

"Did you?"

"No." He raised his head, smiled. He liked this woman. "How do they live?"

"They either try too hard or not hard enough." She pitied them.

"What about your boss?"

"He trying too hard." She sighed.

"When he ask me, should I play for him?"

She laughed. "A little bit for him and a lot for me."

He nodded. "That's a deal."

In a while Reno returned, telling Ludlow the host had asked them to play. There was even a guest who would give them a framework of chords on the piano. As they played, Ludlow did not forget that somewhere near the kitchen the maid was standing, probably on tired feet, listening.

PART FIVE

INTERVIEW . . .

By the time the war was ending, people was liking
the new way we was playing a little bit, and some night
clubs was giving us work. I quit the bands finally and got
my first group together, with Reno, who was driving
hard, getting better with every measure he played. Hardie, overnight he got real good. He just picked up the
whole thing—bang. So he quit O'Gee too and got himself
a pretty good group. People'll always like trombone, you
know; I guess he made more money than any of us.

So, all in all, it was pretty good there for a while. . . .

I

They were still celebrating. Even now, at two in the morning, firecrackers were still exploding, echoing over the city. The club had been noisy and hot. By ten it had become a smoke chamber, as more and more people descended the steps, ordered champagne and lit cigarettes. It was a bad night for playing. The customers did not even pretend to listen. They screamed, cheered, laughed; some even sang. After the set, Ludlow decided to walk around the block before he lost his temper, charged off the stage and strangled the first person who crossed his path. So he had walked alone, his cane picking out the deep ruts in the sidewalk, warning him of the curbs. Sweat had trickled down his sides, had become trapped in the waistband of his undershorts. He had removed his coat and carried it over his arm.

He paused outside of the club, put his coat on, then opened the door. The stale air, the heat, the smoke, the celebration pressed against his face, making him tired and angry. He went down the stairs. The banister was sticky.

"Congratulations, Ludlow." The owner's small hand reached up and massaged his back. "Congratulations." Beyond the owner, a group of people cheered. When their cheer died, Ludlow realized the musicians were playing what, on a normal night, would have been a loud tune.

"What'd I do, man?"

"We won the God damn war! Come on, Ludlow, you knew the war was over. The Japs gave up. The Big Bomb scared hell out of them."

"I know." There was another cheer. Someone in the far corner was blowing a policeman's whistle. "Why they got to come here to celebrate? Suppose to listen to music here."

"What, d'you want to ruin me?" The owner slapped his back. "Come on, it's only one night."

The musicians were struggling. They seemed unable to pull their ideas together.

"Come on, cheer up. Some people over here want to buy you a drink." The owner took his elbow. Even through Ludlow's shirt and suit coat, the hand was fat and soft. They went over to the row of booths. "Here he is, people. I got him." There was a small cheer. The owner went on, "Ludlow, this is my son, Myron. He goes to college." The owner was very proud.

"Glad to know you, Ludlow." Myron's voice was high, lugging even more New York in it than his father's. "Pop, I'm buying Ludlow a drink. All right?"

"Sure, Myron. It's all on me tonight."

"Sit down, Ludlow."

It annoyed him to have Myron call him by his first name. He was not nearly old enough to expect or even want to be called Mister Washington, but he almost wanted it now from Myron.

The owner guided him into the booth. He sat, his thigh press-

153

ing against that of a girl. It was rather a bony thigh, but feeling it warm against him, he was excited nonetheless.

Myron was directly across from him. "So let me introduce you around." Next to Myron was his date, who was giggly and sounded short. In the corner on Ludlow's side was Myron's roommate. Ludlow missed his name, did not care. Between the roommate and Ludlow was the owner of the thigh, a girl named Ragan.

"It's really great about the war, huh?" Myron was leaning into the center of the table, shouting, his breath smelling of liquor and unbrushed teeth.

"What war, Myron?" Ludlow pressed down hard on the name, twisting from it new meanings.

Next to him Ragan shifted her leg, trying to keep from touching him. He shifted with her. "Ain't you got enough room?"

"You shouldn't joke about the war." She was too serious for the din and laughter around her. "My father says that when it's all counted, two hundred fifty thousand soldiers will have been killed—not counting the other side, and the atom bombs and the Jews. You shouldn't joke about the war."

"What's your father, baby, a God-damned general?"

Her voice was cold. "Almost. A colonel."

Ludlow smiled. "Then I guess he knows, all right."

The others had paused uneasily in their conversations, and when finally Myron spoke, it was with a desperate tone. "Well, when do you play again? Do you still have time for a drink?"

"Yeah. If you still want to buy it."

"Of course I do." He fled the booth, saying he would find their waiter and buy cigarettes.

Myron's roommate immediately began questioning Myron's

154

date about the courses she planned to take in the fall. Ludlow drummed calypso rhythm on the table.

"I didn't mean to get so serious." Ragan spoke almost in a whisper, with just the smallest edge of nervousness. She had a nice voice, the pronunciation clear and precise, almost British. Ludlow could not decide what part of the country she might come from, and he was usually quite good at placing accents.

She had given in a bit and he decided he would too. "I wasn't joking about the war." He took a chance, leaned closer. "I was kidding Myron."

She giggled. "I know. . . . Friends? I have my hand out." He liked that. She knew he could not see her hand, had accepted that without being embarrassed by it. He reached out his hand; hers slid into his, squeezed it, then quickly pulled away. Her hand was quite wide for a woman's.

"I'm not sure I understand the way you play. I mean, I like jazz, but I've only heard swing and Dixieland." He could not tell if she was really interested, or if she was simply making talk.

"It's all the same." He shrugged.

"Now you're indulging me." She sounded hurt. "All right then, we'll talk about something else."

He had not intended to hurt her. "Well, it is kinda the same. Just a few different things we doing."

She turned toward him, her knee pressing harder against him. Her breath smelled of lipstick. "Like what?"

He tried as best he could to explain it to her, what they were trying to do. When he had finished, answering her very intelligent questions, repeating things she had not quite understood, she seemed to have gotten it all. It came as a shock to realize

155

there were others in the booth, that Myron had long since returned, that the waiter had brought their drinks.

"So in other words,"—Myron was leaning toward them—"what you're saying is that the difference between modern jazz and the older forms is a sense of time and not just more highly developed technique."

At first he did not understand what the boy was talking about, then realized the others had been listening, had considered it an open conversation. "No, Myron, I didn't say that at all. I said when the measures is metronomizing the choruses, then you got a kind of jazzy music that's working on a three-tone scale, not on a five like most people think. Understand now?"

Beside him, Ragan was shaking.

"Yes . . . Oh, I see." Myron was confused.

Ragan's laughter broke to the surface; she covered herself by explaining she had just seen something absolutely hilarious across the room.

On stage, the alternate group had begun to play its theme. It just slid over the cheering and laughter. Ludlow moved out of the booth. "Well, it been nice talking to you." He aimed his voice directly at Ragan, then extended his hand. She took it, but, as before, released it quickly.

Myron came to his side, patted his back. "I'm glad you sat down with us, Ludlow."

"My pleasure, Myron." He pronounced it My-rone, then turned back to the table. "Hope to meet you again."

There was a general murmur of agreement.

Myron took his elbow. "I'll get you to the stage, Ludlow."

Reno was waiting for him; he did not speak until Myron had departed. "How things on the old plantation, man?"

"There'll be a rebellion soon." Then he was serious. "How'd she look?"

"Nice. Dark hair, dark eyes, and skin white as rice. Maybe had some freckles, but I couldn't see that far in the smoke and all. How'd she sound?"

"Good." He thought about her voice, but, more important, the things she had said. "Good."

"I guess there have to be some!"

The music ended and there were footsteps at the top of the stairs. The musicians pushed by them. One of them stopped, smacked Ludlow's arm. "You can have them, man. I coulda played one note the whole forty minutes. It wouldn'ta mattered."

They played a good set. Ludlow was unable to make a mistake. They even seemed to break into the table-centered world of the celebrants, making some listen. At the end of the set, Ludlow asked Reno to walk him by the booth where Ragan had been.

"What for, man?" Reno hesitated. "They gone."

2

He boarded the subway in Harlem. Dragged and pushed, rattled and shaken, he rode underground listening to the train's rumbling, screeching, knocking, jangling and clicking. Finally the train climbed a grade, went into a curve, crushing him back into the straw seat. The noises untied themselves and spread across the night. The train was outside now, elevated, and in the Bronx. He was going to Hardie's for Christmas dinner.

After it came from underground it made fifteen stops. When he got off, the car was silent and empty. The platform was wooden. A cold wind tore across the open elevated station.

"Ludlow! Merry Christmas!" Hardie's footsteps ran toward him down the platform. Ludlow had been traveling; he had not spoken to Hardie in almost six months.

"Merry Christmas, man." Ludlow extended his hand. "How you been?"

Hardie's hand was cold and chapped. "Fine! Fine. Can't complain about nothing."

"How Juanita and the boy?" Hardie was guiding him down steel-rimmed steps, through a clicking turnstile of cold, smooth wood.

"They fine, man."

They descended more steps and were on the street. A few blocks away and high above, the train rumbled toward the city line at Mount Vernon. It had snowed, turned warm, then gone below freezing. The streets were icy. "How the new group working out?"

"Good, man. Keep it quiet but I may have to get a new drummer." Hardie had taken his elbow. "The one I got still keeping bass-drum time."

The hardened snow, the ice crunched underfoot. They walked slowly along the empty street. In some of the houses they passed, radios and phonographs played Christmas songs. In a few hours Ludlow would have to go back into the city to work.

"Well, we made it. God damn ice!" Hardie gripped his elbow a little tighter. "I tried to clean the steps before the freeze, but they still slippery. Got to put salt down." They climbed the brick steps. Hardie jingled coins and keys in his pocket. "Remember down home? How warm it was on Christmas?"

Ludlow nodded. Hardie opened the door; warm air, smelling of turkey and mince pie, met them.

"Come in, man. One step up." They left the cold brick steps for warm wood, then carpet. "Hey, baby, we here!"

A few rooms away, Juanita called back. "Okay. Give him a drink." She began to whisper. Finally, again in a normal voice, "Now run."

Hardie took his coat, led him into the living room, and told him to sit down. Then the trombone player crossed the room, opened cabinets and broke ice. "Here." He handed Ludlow a drink, sat down across from him. "How long, baby?"

"Just take it easy, Hardie." Under Juanita's voice, fat began to pop and sizzle.

Hardie sighed. "So tell me, how'd the tour go?"

"You know. You play, get in a car, ride all night, sleep some, play, then ride some more. I'm sure glad I don't got to drive, but Reno's a God damn maniac."

"Did you know Danny Price run into a tree last month?" Danny Price had been the drummer when they were together with O'Gee.

Ludlow shook his head; he had liked Danny.

"They figure he musta fell asleep."

They were silent for a moment. Ludlow found himself counting the number of musicians he had known who had died in automobile accidents. He had reached nine when Juanita clicked into the room, smelling of perfume and turkey.

"Merry Christmas, Ludlow." She kissed him on the cheek. "How you been?"

"All right, sweetie." He could not stop thinking about Danny. They had played many after-hour sessions together. Later, Ludlow had used him at a few recording dates.

Juanita sat beside him, squeezed his hand. "Did Hardie take you around the house?" Ludlow had never visited them. They had bought the house less than a year before.

"Not yet." He shook the sound of Danny Price's drums out of his head.

"Too bad it's not spring. We got a garden out back. In the spring, you come up and we'll eat some fried chicken out there."

"All right." He sipped his drink.

Quick, light footsteps came into the room. "Mama?"

"Otie, you bring what I told you?" Juanita pulled forward and let go Ludlow's hand.

"Yes, Mama."

"Well, come on then."

The footsteps scuffled slowly toward him, stopped a few feet away. "Merry Christmas . . ." Otis Hardie, junior, was shy.

"Merry Christmas, Uncle Ludlow." Juanita's voice was warm and sweet, coaxing him.

"Merry Christmas, Uncle Ludlow." The boy pushed a box into Ludlow's hands. "Mama, his eyes are white!"

"Otie!" "Otis!" Juanita and Hardie spoke at the same time. Then Juanita turned to him. "Oh, Ludlow, I'm—"

"It all right, Juanita." He smiled. "He just like you—calls it like he see it. Remember that time in Chicago when Hardie couldn't shut you up?" He spoke now to Otie. "That's because I can't see. That bother you?"

"No. You didn't open your present."

Ludlow extended the box. "You do it and tell me what it is."

The boy came closer, stood between Ludlow's knees and attacked the tissue paper. He smelled of sugar and vaseline. "It's an ashes tray. I made it myself."

"I ain't never had my own ash tray before." It was of rough, dry clay, with a bowl no bigger than Ludlow's thumb.

"He good with his hands." Hardie, still hurt for Ludlow, was nevertheless very proud.

"I bet. You used to be good with your hands too."

Juanita understood first. "That's what I worry about when he goes on the road." She pretended suspicion.

"He all right, Juanita."

"Sure I am, baby." Hardie was too serious.

Juanita laughed. "Just as long as I don't find out about it, I don't care."

Hardie changed the subject. "He really is good with his hands. Come here, son." The boy left Ludlow. "You think you can show your Uncle Ludlow what I taught you?" The boy must have nodded. "Good boy!" Hardie got up and the man and boy crossed the room. There was a piano in the corner. "Okay now."

The boy played. Out of time, with many mistakes, but still recognizable, he played one of Ludlow's tunes, a ballad, *Cherry Tree*. When he finished, they applauded.

Juanita stood up. "Let's go wash up, Otie." She and the boy left the room.

"We might as well go in and sit down." Hardie came back from the piano and stood before him.

In the dining room, Hardie insisted that Ludlow sit at the head. Hardie sat on his right. When Juanita and Otie returned, she sat at the other end, the boy on Ludlow's left.

Juanita brought the plates from the kitchen already served. Hardie told Ludlow where the food was on his plate. Juanita was a good cook and Ludlow told her so.

"Thank you. It all right, Hardie?"

"You see me eating, don't you?" His mouth was full. "Hey, man, remember that Christmas dinner we ate in that diner in Portland?"

"Yeah."

"When was this?" Juanita asked.

"Just after we got married, baby. I left you in Chicago, remember? Did I miss you!"

"I missed you too. I'd sit by the phone and Mama'd come and tell me to eat something and I'd say I couldn't take the chance you'd call and think I was out. I'd get that phone on the first ring."

The gravy had turkey livers and nuts in it.

"That how come you picked it up so fast?"

"That's how come." Her fork rang on her plate; she had put it down.

"Let go my hand, baby. Got to catch up to Ludlow." His voice swung Ludlow's way. "Look at him go!"

"Good food." He was wishing he had not let Hardie seat him at the end.

"Otie, don't play with your food!" Juanita moved her chair. "Now, I'm watching you, young man."

"He look tired, baby. I guess opening all them boxes wore him out."

"Maybe so." She paused a moment. "Maybe I'll take him up to bed."

"Why don't you do that."

"Come on, Otis-motis." She got up. The boy's chair pushed back from the table. "Say good night to everybody."

"Good night, Daddy."

"Night, son."

"Good night . . ."

"Uncle Ludlow," Juanita coached.

"Uncle Ludlow."

Juanita did not return before they had finished dinner. Hardie had gone to find out what was keeping her, and returned, reporting that Otie, overstuffed, overexcited, and overtired, had vomited all over his pillow.

When it was time for Ludlow to leave, Hardie walked him to the subway. Hardie had planned to stay with him until the train arrived, but Ludlow persuaded him to go home to his family. It was ten minutes before the train pulled into the station, dousing his face with cold wind, and took him into the city to work.

3

He had always liked Tuesday night. Very few people came to night clubs in the middle of the week, but those who came did so to sit quietly over a drink and listen. Tuesday night was not good for owners, but it was very good for musicians.

He had done some of his best playing on Tuesday, especially with ballads. This Tuesday he had just finished his fourth set, acknowledged the almost timid applause, and was now descending the steps. He wanted a drink.

The hand which touched his coat sleeve was large and heavy. "Excuse me, Mister Washington? Do you remember me? Myron's friend, Ragan?" The whispering voice was faintly familiar, and he thought rapidly over the last few weeks attempting to fix it exactly, but for the moment could not.

"Sure, I do. How you been?" If a woman approached a man and asked if he remembered her, he always said he did.

"No, you don't at all." She did not seem upset about it. "But it's nice of you to say so."

He tried to identify her accent. But she had none. He had met a girl without an accent the night the war ended. "I really do. Your old man's a colonel in the army. Ain't that so?"

She laughed. "Well, I just wanted to say I enjoyed your playing, especially the slow things . . . I have my hand out."

He took her hand. "How about me buying you and your date a drink?" He did not relish the idea of buying some college boy a drink, but he needed time to find out what the girl had in mind, why she had gone out of her way to stop and praise him.

"I don't have a date." She drew a breath as if to continue, but did not.

This was too easy to be true. "Well, then I'll buy you a drink." He smiled, still holding her hand. "Just get us to the bar."

At the bar, they climbed onto stools and ordered, listening to the alternate group until the drinks arrived.

"Last time I did all the talking." He turned on his stool until his knee was poking into her thigh. She did not move, but he was beginning to doubt that she really understood what was happening. Sometimes white people confused him. He could not always assume they knew the signals. "So now it's your turn to talk."

"That question always mixes me up. I never know where to start. What do you want me to tell about?"

He rested one elbow on the bar and scratched his ear. "How come you night-clubbing without no date. Your folks wouldn't like that."

"I wanted to hear you play. I'm a big fan of yours now. And I couldn't wait around for someone to call and ask me to go out. As for my parents, they're in France."

"And what you doing here?"

"I went to college here and now I have a job here."

He nodded, admiring how she spoke, her voice. He did not

like the usual white girl who went with Negro musicians. Their attempts to speak like Negroes annoyed, angered him. There was more than a scent of condescension in their attempts. Now, listening to this girl, he resented the others more than ever. "You like your job?"

"It's all right, I guess. Maybe later I'll do something else." She was vague about this and he realized that to pursue it would only make her uneasy.

He sighed and sat up straight. "You understand what we was doing tonight?"

"I think so. You made it very clear, and now I have some of your records to practice-listen to." She swallowed, set her glass on the bar. "You'll think I'm trying to pick you up, I know, but would you like to take a ride in the country when you finish work? I have a convertible."

Ludlow almost fell backward off the stool. "Why sure. That'd be nice." He was very confused now. She was either the most innocent woman he had never met, or the most forward. He was sure that it was innocence. He would have to rearrange his entire approach.

When the club closed at four, she led him to her car. He slid across leather seats; through his shoes, he felt thick carpeting. "Colonels don't make this much, do they?"

She laughed. "No. My father got it before the war." She started the motor, shifted into gear, and steered into the light traffic. It was early spring, still quite cool in the mornings. After a few stops, and fast starts, he felt the absence of the wind-breaking buildings and knew they were near the river, driving fast. He turned up the collar of his suitcoat. The ride was more refreshing than sleep. He could almost feel the seven hours of stale air easing out of his lungs. Fresh air burned in his throat, as if he had been sucking mints.

They left the city and entered the suburbs; the trees snapped by at the roadside and muffled the rushing wind. They had a chance to talk without shouting.

"I can't see your face, but I bet you like driving."

"Yes, I do." It was a squeal. Then she became more serious. "Whenever I get upset about something, I get in the car and leave it behind."

"What upsets you?" It was an important question; the answer would help him to formulate plans.

She held back her laughter. "Oh, well, just any old trauma."

He did not know what she meant, but responded quickly, attempting to disarm her. "Don't use such big words, college girl."

"Okay, man." She tried to imitate him, knew she had not succeeded, and laughed at her attempt. He laughed too.

No tires but theirs buzzed against the pavement; no cars passed them, wavelike. Their motor alone echoed against the wall of trees. Then he was thrown forward as she braked and turned off the highway. After a few minutes, gravel popped and pelted the fenders. Finally she stopped, and cut off the motor. For a moment there was nothing, and then, as his ears became accustomed to the stillness, he realized she had stopped on the shore of a small pond.

"Where the hell'd you bring me?" He whispered so as not to disturb the quiet.

"My place."

"You own it?" He could not believe this.

"Only by payments of love and time."

At first he did not understand what she meant. Finally he realized she was saying that she liked to come there often.

"Would you like to throw some rocks into my pond?" Before he could answer, her door opened and she was crunching gravel, her steps as rapid as a running child, around to his side. "Come on." She opened his door, took his hand and helped him out.

She guided him forward ten steps. "Don't move from that spot or you'll get your shoes wet. Here." She thrust some rocks into his hand. "Now, listen." She grunted and after a few seconds, over the lapping, a splash came from the distant water. "Now it's your turn."

He had never learned to throw very well and his stone did not take as long to fall as had hers.

When they had lobbed all their stones, she whispered, "Don't move and you'll be able to feel the moon kiss your skin."

Ludlow did not understand any of this, but still, it enchanted him. He wished she would move closer so he might kiss her, but she remained always at least ten feet from him, and, not knowing the terrain, he was afraid to move. He did not want to find himself knee-deep in cold water. He laughed at the idea.

She was annoyed, hurt. "What's funny?"

He decided to tell her, certain that even if he angered her, she would still drive him home. "I'm thinking if I knew where the hell we was, and if I was sure I wouldn't end up taking a cold bath, I'd come over and kiss you, because . . ." he started to laugh, "because, baby, you sure ain't making no moves toward me!"

She laughed too, then a lid clamped down on her laughter. The gravel rustled and he smelled perfume. "Here I am."

He put his arms around her and kissed her, measuring her body by feeling it against his own. She came to his nose and was thin, except for her breasts, which, bound by a tight, high bra, were large. Her shoulders were broad, bony and square; her waist was thin enough to encircle with his hands. "Well, well, well. . . ."

By the way she kissed, hungry and tight-lipped at the same time, he knew she was ready—knew, if he simply wanted to have a white girl, he could push her down on the sharp, small stones underfoot and make love to her. But then she would be ashamed of herself and he would never meet her again—and he wanted very much to meet her again, wanted to know her. He had never in his life met anyone like her. He kissed her a few more times, stroked her breasts once, then gently pushed her away.

She was breathing deeply, evenly. He put his fingers to her face, found her mouth small and slightly open, stunned. Her forehead was broad, her jaw square, her chin pointed.

"Come on, baby, you better take me home." He spoke to her in much the way he would have spoken to a child.

"All right," she whispered, trancelike.

She drove slower now. The air was moist, slightly warm. There were more cars. "Where you live?"

She told him the address, in the Fifties on the East side. "I can walk to work."

"You got a roommate or something?" He realized she would know he was collecting information to find out whose bed they would eventually use, but he also wanted to know about her, about her life.

"No."

He shook his head. "No date, no roommate. You got any friends?"

"Just a few."

"Well, how the hell you ever meet a fuck-up like Myron?" He shifted toward her.

"The other girl was a friend of mine in college."

In all she had said, in the way she spoke, in her precise, whispering voice, there was a quality of resignation, almost of doom. He could not have named it, but he recognized it. "Get off this highway and stop somewhere." It was an order. He wanted her full attention.

She took the next exit, drove along winding, pitted streets and finally parked. When she killed the motor, there was a radio, probably in someone's bedroom, playing classical music. Directly above him in a rustling tree, two birds twittered.

"What the hell kind of life you been leading?"

She said nothing for a long while. Then only one word: "Lonely."

He moved closer to her, and, twisting toward her, rested his right elbow on the steering wheel. "Well, no more." She did not move. "You hear me? Not no more. Them days is gone." He reached out, took her chin between his thumb and index finger, turned her face toward him and kissed her.

She put a hand on his cheek, but still did not speak.

He smiled and turned front again. "Okay, now let's go to Harlem and get some eggs and grits."

4

They had breakfast in a restaurant on Amsterdam Avenue, the jukebox, even at the start of the day, blaring mostly rhythm-and-blues or Inez Cunningham, but sometimes something by Hardie or Ludlow. From the kitchen came the smells of greens, black-eyed peas and pork. Near the front window ribs sizzled on the barbeque rack. The local numbers man held court there, and often, while they ate, the door opened, footsteps crossed to the booth behind them, a number would be whispered, and money would jingle on the wooden table.

Ragan came to hear him that night and every night for weeks after and most times they would drive until morning, always talking, unburdening themselves. She told him about the succession of army camps in which she had grown up, the constant moving, the sad, abrupt endings to friendships just begun; she told him about the loneliness. He spoke of his marriage and why he thought it had not worked and about the long, sometimes exciting years, afterward. He had never before thought of himself as having been lonely, but realized now, with wonder, that was what he had been. He considered himself lucky to have discovered he had been lonely only after he was no longer lonely.

When finally they made love, in her apartment with Inez Cunningham singing for them on the phonograph, and the early morning sun's heat baking them, it came without planning or preparation. They had driven there for breakfast before she had to go to work, had slumped full-bellied on the sofa to talk. Then next, they were naked, their arms tightly around each other.

One day, in the middle of August, he pushed himself far inside her, grabbed her shoulders, sighed, and surprising himself, told her he loved her. She said she had loved him for months but had been afraid to tell him.

It was late September now and getting colder. When they drove, the air hinted at winter and, along the highways around the city, was heavy with the smoke of smoldering leaves. They still made love with the window open, but now under a light blanket.

She grabbed him tightly, then sighed. "Oh, my."

"What's the matter?" His arms were around her waist, his leg between hers.

"In about three hours I have to go to work." Her lips brushed, then kissed his shoulder.

"Well, you know, you'll just have to up and marry me. Then you won't have to work, just have babies."

"I guess I'll have to do that." Her kiss made his ear pop. "I love you, Ludlow."

"I love you too, baby." He did not like the way these words came from him. He had never wanted anything he had ever said to sound as sincere, but still these words always seemed empty to

172

him, as if the words themselves reared up to remind him of all the insincere and selfish things he had ever done.

Her nose was cold; she pressed it against his chest. "I want to make a confession." She was not too serious.

"Go on." He smiled. "Who was he?"

"No one, Ludlow. Never." The idea of her making love to anyone else made her very serious.

"Okay." He patted her back, ran his hand over a protruding shoulder blade.

"I came to see you five times before I spoke to you."

"When?"

"The night we drove to my pond." She sounded insecure now. "You remember that night, don't you?"

"Sure I do."

"Well, I came five times and each time I promised myself I'd talk to you, but I never did."

"Why not?" He had never understood when women confessed such things to him. They always seemed to mean absolutely nothing to him, but so much to them.

"I was afraid of you."

"Afraid of a little old blind man?"

He felt her head nodding. "Because I really did like you and I wanted you so much to like me. Not many people did, you know." This did not upset her particularly; there was nothing more than resignation in her whispering voice.

"Now you got lots of friends."

"I know. It's wonderful." She paused, rolling away from him a few inches. It seemed a mile. A breeze cooled the sweat on his stomach. "We haven't talked much about the world, Ludlow . . . and what I'm going to say now may seem crazy. I know it's mystical! But I think Negroes know how I feel about you."

"Sure they do. They see you with me all the time." He reached out, found her head and ruffled her hair, cut almost as short as a boy's.

"No, Ludlow, you don't understand." She turned onto her stomach, crawled closer, and on top of him, her voice coming down now. "I mean, Negroes who don't know you, or even me. I mean, like the janitor where I work is a Negro and whenever he sees me he just beams. He never looked at me before I met you. It's like he knows I love you and he's glad for me. That sounds really silly, doesn't it."

"No it don't, baby." Speaking at first to reassure her, he realized it was certainly possible. Perhaps Negroes could see in her face that she had somehow chosen to cast her lot with them. "Could be true, Ragan."

"I know it's true!" For an instant she was quite excited, then her head fell onto his chest. "I'd better get some sleep."

He did not want to sleep; he wanted to make love to her, and moved his hand across the small of her back.

"What're you doing?" She knew perfectly well, and did not have to wait for an answer. "Ludlow, don't now. If I don't get these few hours I'll fall asleep on my desk." She wiggled her buttocks.

Finally she slid full on top of him, and kissed him furiously. After a few moments, he rolled her over. But before they could make love, he had to stop and reach for the small tin on the bed table.

When he had first known her, Ragan's shoulders had bothered him. They were too hard, the bones and joints seeming about to tear through the soft skin. They were the shoulders of a frightened child tensed for a blow it cannot avoid. One day, he had realized his own shoulders must have tensed the same way when

174

the Warden's assistant was about to whip him. After that, her shoulders no longer bothered him; they became important to him, for they told what her life had been and how much better he had made it. Usually, her shoulders were not tense when they finished making love. Now, lying on top of her, he cupped his hands gently around them.

She held him under the armpits. "Am I really as good as they are?"

He kissed her. "They who?"

"The Negro girls you've made love to. Your wife." She had asked him this often and he could not seem to convince her that Negro women had no special natural power, that it was only a matter of an attitude.

"My ex-wife. Sure you are, baby. I don't keep no lists anyway."

"I'm glad I'm better. I want to make you forget everyone else."

"You do."

"Good. Now you have to get off me so I can go to work." He rolled away from her. She followed him and kissed him softly. "I love you."

He remained in bed while she took a shower, dressed, made coffee, and cooked breakfast. She brought the food and put it on the bed table. "Oh, God, let me get rid of this terrible thing." She scurried to the bathroom and flushed the toilet.

He was sitting up when she returned. "I'm walking you to work." He pushed down the covers, and swung his feet onto the floor.

"But you have to get some sleep."

"I been without sleep before." He found his undershorts and pulled them on.

"I think you should stay here, Ludlow. How'll you get back?" She was concerned.

175

"I been moving all over this city for ten years . . . just me and my cane." He bragged, buttoning his shirt.

She said no more about it, and said very little otherwise. They finished breakfast, stacked the dishes in the sink, and left her apartment.

"Something wrong, Ragan?" She had been too quiet, even for her.

"You'll be hurt if I tell you." She was speaking down toward the pavement. They were nearing the big street on which she worked. It was difficult to pick up her voice over the morning traffic.

"Maybe. You tell me anyway."

"I didn't want you to walk with me today."

He stopped her. People brushed by them. "Why not?"

"I wanted to be alone, that's all." She was almost whining.

"You coulda told me that, baby. I told you once you could tell me everything. Ain't nothing'll shock me."

"I didn't want to hurt your feelings."

All at once, he could never learn why, he was suspicious. "You sure there ain't nothing else?" He realized his voice sounded hard.

"No. There is nothing else." She was nervous.

He shrugged, laughed. "Well, it too late now for you to be alone. I might as well walk you all the way."

"No!" She fairly shouted, panic coating her words. "Look, I'm late now, Ludlow. We can talk about this later. But I'd better leave you here. Bye-bye." She squeezed his hand and released it. Her heels disappeared behind a blaring horn.

He gripped his cane so tightly his hand began to hurt. Suspicion was shrill in his head, a clarinet played by a shaky old man. She did not want him to walk her to the door of her office build-

176

ing because she did not want her office friends to know about him. She wanted to keep him on some side street of her life, like Negro mistresses were always kept on side streets by their lovers. She had met all his friends, Hardie, Reno, even Norman Spencer; he had met none of hers.

He knew where she worked. He would follow her, go to the receptionist and say he wanted to speak to her. He would say he was her husband. He could imagine the gasp the receptionist would make. The news would travel throughout her building in less than a minute—about nice, quiet little Ragan and her blind nigger husband. Standing in the middle of the sidewalk, people rushing by him on either side, he rivaled the noise of the passing automobiles with his laughter.

But then he realized he did not want revenge; he wanted Ragan. If she did not really want him, revenge would make him feel no better. He decided to return to her place, wait for her and bring it all into the open.

He was prepared to wait until after five, but she rushed in a few minutes after noon. Before he could ready himself, she was on the floor in front of his chair, the sound of her crying muffled in his thighs. He tried to be stern, but could not and stroked her hair. "What's wrong, baby?"

"I was so . . . so . . . cowardly this morning . . . and mean!" She continued to cry, but softer now.

"About what?" Perhaps she would tell him without being questioned and he would not have to reveal his suspicions.

"About your walking with me. I just left you standing there."

"Well, why didn't you want me to walk you?" He was stroking her neck now. Her breasts were pressed against his shins.

"Because . . . oh, Ludlow, don't . . . because I was meeting a friend of my parents."

177

It was true. He realized now that though he had thought his suspicions possible, he had not thought them true. "Well . . ."

She wrapped her arms around his calves and squeezed them tightly, her sobs jolting both of them. "Yesterday I got permission to come to work an hour late this morning. But this morning I still had to go to work—I mean, to the building—because I was meeting my parents' friend in the lobby."

He was shaking his head. She began to talk much faster now. "He's going to France and he'll be seeing my parents and he called me at work yesterday and asked me to meet him this morning because his plane was leaving at noon. So I said yes. But then you wanted to walk me and I got panicked he'd be there and see us and tell them and I didn't want to tell them yet —they're good people really, but I want to tell them myself, and gently. You understand that, don't you?"

He had taken his hands from her head, was digging with his little finger in his ear. "Look, Ragan, I don't want to know this." He leaned back.

"No, wait, Ludlow, listen—please listen." He wished she would stop. "Please listen. So we went for coffee and I must've looked terrible. I know I felt terrible. I knew I'd betrayed you. And finally he asked me what was wrong." She paused. "And I started to cry, and—oh Ludlow, please listen—I told him every-thing."

His stomach dropped; he felt warm. "Everything what?"

"I told him everything. And I told him to tell my parents. That you're a Negro, that you're blind, that you're a musician, and that I love you. I told him."

He was leaning forward now, almost afraid to believe her. "What'd he say?"

She laughed shrilly. "Oh, he asked me if I was insane. And I

178

said no. That all my life I'd been lonely and frightened and now I loved you and wasn't any of those things any more." She stopped. "I love you very much, Ludlow."

He covered her ears with his hands, bent forward and kissed her. "I love you too." Then, taking her under the arms, he helped her up and onto his lap. Pulling up her blouse, he unfastened her bra and cupped his hand over her breast. She rested her head on his shoulder. After a few minutes he asked her, whispering, when she had to return to work, but she had fallen fast asleep.

5

They decided to live together and moved into three furnished rooms and a kitchen on the upper West side, Ludlow's first real home since he had left New Marsails. When he finished working, they would go straight to their apartment and Ragan would fix him breakfast. She had never made grits before, but learned. She still went to work, and slept in the late afternoons so they could be together as much as possible. A few Sundays in autumn they drove to the Bronx and sat in Hardie's back yard until the cold-edged breeze forced them into the house to dinner. But for some reason Ragan did not like going to the Bronx and they did not go often.

The New Music, as it was called, had now caught on, and people all over the country wanted to hear it played by those who had done the most to create it. *Four-Four* magazine, which had early given Ludlow recognition, organized a nationwide concert tour built around Ludlow, Hardie, and a few others.

The night before they left, the four of them—Hardie, Juanita,

Ragan and Ludlow—ate dinner together, then went to Harlem to listen to Norman Spencer.

"I want to make a toast." Ludlow let go Ragan's hand and picked up his glass. "To the ladies—who make life good."

"Which ladies?" Juanita sat to his left. They were at a small circular table.

"You two—what you think?"

"Just so you keep it that way." She was being too serious. "Someday I'll go on tour."

"What'll you do, baby?" Hardie must have been resting on his forearms; his voice was only a few inches from the table.

"I don't know, but I'll find something to tour with."

Hardie straightened up. "You better just stay home with Otie."

"All right, baby." She was very sweet now. Ludlow listened to the small kiss.

"To the ladies?" Ludlow extended his glass, felt Hardie's click against his. They drank.

He turned to Ragan. "How you doing?"

"All right." She was sad, had said very little this evening.

"Awh, baby, I'll be back." He spoke to Juanita and Hardie. "She thinks I ain't coming back."

"He's coming back, Ragan. I'll bring him back myself. And you know I'm coming back."

Ludlow put his arm around Ragan's shoulder, felt her raise her head. She was a little happier now, but not much. "All right."

He appealed to Juanita. "Now won't we be coming back? Don't Hardie always come back?"

"Yes."

He had expected more from her than one word. "Now what's wrong with you?"

"Not a thing." She did not mean it, then suddenly she brightened. "Nothing wrong with me. I'm getting rid of my husband for a couple months."

"You sound like you mean that." Hardie was puzzled.

"Do I?" She laughed. "All right, we'll forget about it. How'd this conversation start anyway? Oh, yesss." She paused. "Don't worry, Ragan, Ludlow'll come back." Her voice was flat.

"You see, baby? It'll be all right."

"All right."

They did not stay much longer. The four sat silently in the car as Hardie drove Ludlow and Ragan home. The closing doors echoed down the quiet street. A few blocks away, cars washed along the highway.

Ludlow stood beside the car, the cold coming through the soles of his shoes. In one of his coat pockets, he and Ragan held hands.

"I'll pick you up at eleven, right?" Hardie's voice came up from the car window.

"Good." Ludlow felt Ragan squeeze his hand. Her smooth fingernails were colder than the rest of her hand.

"I guess I won't be seeing you, Ragan, but I'll take care of Ludlow for you." She did not answer. "You take care of yourself. So long."

Ludlow nodded, stepping back. The car's exhaust smelled salty.

Upstairs, that morning's bacon and coffee still hung in the air of the apartment. As soon as they had closed the door and removed their heavy overcoats, Ragan grabbed him around the ribs and pressed against him. She was shaking. "Promise you'll come back. Promise."

He could not help smiling, but did so with his chin resting on the top of her head so she would not see it and be hurt. "I promise, baby. I'll come back like a God damn homing pigeon."

"No, Ludlow. Don't joke. Promise."

"I'll come back, Ragan. I promise."

She released him, stepped away. She must have been looking at him. "All right." She led him into the bedroom, hugged him again. "I love you, Ludlow. I don't know if I'll be able to do without you for three months." She could have been smiling now. "I'll probably end up in Los Angeles one night."

"That'd be nice."

"Do you really love me?" She was worried.

"I love you all right."

She stood on tiptoe to kiss him, her breasts rubbing against him. "I'll write you every day . . . I won't be able to say everything I'd like to because Hardie will see, but I'll write."

He pushed her back, and reached for the buttons on her blouse—cold, of metal, with a design stamped on them. She stood and did not move, her hands at her sides, until he had removed all her clothes. "Get under the covers, girl. Don't want to leave you here sniffling."

Her quick, bare steps went across the room. The covers rustled.

He took off his coat, pulled at his tie. "There a couple things in the drawer there?"

She did not answer immediately, nor did she open the drawer of the bed table. "Ludlow, I don't want anything at all between us, not even something that thin. Not tonight."

He thought a moment. "Where you at?"

Now she did move—opened the drawer, fanned through the pages of a book, her diary. She counted, whispering, then sighed. "I may not be . . ." She did not finish.

"Where you at?" He took a step closer to the bed, continuing to undress, dropping his clothes on a nearby chair.

"Right in the middle." She crawled across the bed, toward him, and grabbed his hands. "I can't stand the idea of that thing tonight."

Someday they would get married. In fact, sometimes he did not know why they were not already married. They had always been very careful because they wanted to choose the time to marry and have children. But then, even if she were to become pregnant, he would never feel forced into marrying her. If he wanted, he could always arrange an abortion anyway. But he would not even want to arrange one; he would want to marry her and feel her grow large and have his child. He would be able to feel something for a child now, especially hers. He decided: no matter what happened, it could not turn out badly. "All right, Ragan." He laughed. "We'll play this number without a mute."

He was undressed now. When he got into bed, she wrapped her thin arms and legs around him as if she intended never to let him go.

6

    She wrote him every day for two months. Then finally she missed a day. He did not worry. It had probably been luck that he received all of her letters, especially since the tour spent no more than three days in any one city. But in a week, he still had received no word and he began to grow concerned. He tried to call her several times, but she was never at home, the phone buzzing until the operator apologized. He had Hardie call Juanita and ask her to contact Ragan. In a few days Juanita wrote saying she had called and even gone by, but had found no one.

    He was tempted to leave the tour that day, but he did not. It was going very well; sell-out crowds were coming to hear them, him really, and he realized that twenty men were depending on him. Anxiously he waited for the tour to end and then, as quickly as possible, returned to New York.

    As his taxi turned into their street, he did not know what to expect. He might find her gone and the place empty, echoing, no furniture to swallow the sound of his footsteps or voice. But if she had left him, she probably would have written him. Perhaps he might even find her lying on the floor, dead, the victim of some crime, the blood from the blows on her head crusty now, the room smelling sweet. He began to shake as the narrow elevator carried him to their floor.

He put down his instrument case and bag, found the key, and opened the door. If she was gone, she had not been gone long; her perfume was still strong in the rooms. He moved his bags over the threshold, closed the door, and stepped across the squeaking, carpetless floor.

Rapid steps came toward him, and, thinking he might have surprised a thief, he ducked from them, but then: "Oh, Ludlow . . ." She was hanging on him, moaning as he himself had moaned his first day at the Home; she moaned and repeated his name.

"What's wrong, Ragan?" He held the back of her neck, kissed her mouth; it tasted of tears, of being hungry. "What's the trouble?"

She only moaned, hugging him. He led her into the living room, to the sofa. They sat down. She moaned on his shoulder. Even though he knew something terrible must have happened, he was happy. The worst had not happened; she had not left him.

He waited until she showed signs of quieting. "What's the trouble?"

She put her arms around his neck. "I'm so glad to see you."

"Why'd you stop writing?"

"I—couldn't. I—" She did not finish, began to gasp, fighting tears. "I didn't know what to do. I couldn't get anyone to help me."

"With what?"

"At first I couldn't believe it. I didn't want to believe it." She sighed. "I didn't know what to do."

He fought being impatient with her. "About what?"

"I'm—I'm preg—nant." The second half of the word shook from her.

He could not understand why she was so upset. They had figured that risk into their decision to make love that night.

"Ludlow, what'll we do? I tried to find a doctor, but I couldn't —I mean, to do something, but there was some trouble. I mean, another doctor, he couldn't tell if I was really pregnant or if I had been and it was dead. I mean, they couldn't tell me any-thing and I couldn't find anyone and—what'll we do?"

The answer was so simple, but he hesitated to say it. "Don't worry, Ragan." He put his arm around her.

"But I'm almost three months pregnant!" Suddenly she had stopped crying; no trace of it remained in her dry, brittle whisper.

He would have to give her the answer, though he wished she had thought of it alone. "We'll get married, is all." He laughed nervously. "So we did things a little ass-backwards."

She did not reply for a long moment. "We can't do that, Lud-low." Rather than a flat refusal, it was resignation to a sad fact.

"But, baby, we was always getting married. So what if you have a baby three months too soon. Who'll know? And who'll really care?"

"You don't understand." She was slightly annoyed.

He put his hands on her shoulders and turned her toward him, kissed her. "You got pregnant that night we—"

"Don't say it!" Her hands covered her ears.

He grabbed her wrists and pulled them down so she would have to listen. "We knew what we was doing. You looked in your book, right? You said you was in the middle of the month, dangerous time, right? I said to myself: so what if she get a baby. I love her. I'll want her to have it. So what's the difference? You ain't got to wear no sign around your neck telling your baby was born six months after you got married."

"I'm not worried about that, Ludlow." Her shoulders swayed; she was shaking her head slowly.

"Well, what then?"

"I don't want you to feel forced into marrying me."

"But, Ragan, ain't nobody forcing me. We love each other, right?" He waited for the answer.

"Yes." He did not like the tone in her voice, as if she might be having doubts.

He ignored this and went on: "We was planning to get married sooner or later, right?"

"Yes."

"What's changed?" He tried to think as she must be thinking, and asked again the only question he could find. "You think people'll be counting the months between when we get married to when you have a baby?" He shook his head. "Ragan-honey, people don't give two shits about other people."

She began to shake, but, he soon discovered, not with crying. "I am not thinking about other people! I'm thinking about us."

"So'm I." He was bewildered.

"No, you're not!" She was becoming angry. "I don't want you to turn around in a year or two and feel trapped."

An uneasy, sick feeling was pursuing and overtaking him. "I don't neither, Ragan."

"But you don't understand." She sighed, began reluctantly. "I've been sitting here alone for almost a week realizing things

I never realized before." She twisted her wrists out of his grip. "We're very different, Ludlow."

"I know that."

"I mean, you know what you want out of life. You want to play music. But I'm just realizing I don't know at all what I want to do. Suppose someday I want to do something you don't want me to do?"

"But everybody take that chance, Ragan."

"It's wrong to take it. It's not fair to you."

"I'll decide what's fair for me."

"Anyway, that's why we can't get married."

She was not being realistic and he had to help her to be. She had lost touch with all the things they had taken for granted. "Well, what you planning to do if we don't get married? Ain't it getting too late to get rid of it?"

"I don't know what I'll do, Ludlow. Don't nag me."

"I ain't nagging you, baby. I'm just trying to get you to do the best thing for us."

"You mean the best thing for you." She took a deep breath, sighed, took another breath. "Ludlow, I don't want to get married now. I don't want to have a baby. I'm not ready to be a mother." Her voice was cold.

Perhaps if he got a little tough; it sometimes worked with her. "Ready or not, baby, you'll be a mama in six months."

She got up, walked across the room, stopped, turned around. "Don't rub it in."

"I ain't rubbing it in. I'm just trying to make you und—"

"Ludlow, I don't want to get married."

Somehow they had to get back to the essentials of the situation, of their lives. "Ragan, don't you love me?" There was a long silence, too long, and he began to sweat.

"I don't know, Ludlow." He ducked as if to avoid a blow. She went on: "I did before. I mean, I suppose I still do, Ludlow, honestly. But now everything's different. I mean, I don't think I realized before all the things loving you meant."

He had been cut so deeply his nerves had been severed; he was numb. "You mean all this time you been playing around, lying to me?"

"No." She might be crying now. "No, Ludlow. Lying to myself maybe." She appealed to him. "Don't you understand? I don't know what to do. I don't want to hurt you and I'm afraid I will if we get married."

He no longer wanted to hurt her. "That's my worry, Ragan. I love you. I ain't never loved nobody, not even when I was married before. I didn't even know what love was. But now I do and if you marry me, I'll love that baby you'll have." He was pleading with her and did not care. Then, all at once, he knew the real reason why she did not want to marry him. "You worrying about your folks, ain't you."

She did not answer immediately. "My parents?" She sounded guilty.

He nodded. "Don't worry about them, Ragan. They can't do nothing to you. And when they understand how much we love each other, they be all right. And besides, it ain't like they don't know nothing at all about us, because you told their friend that time."

Her whisper was so soft it took longer than usual to reach his brain. He had already begun to speak again.

"I didn't tell him."

"So they know all about me and what I do and—what?"

"I didn't tell them anything." Her voice was a bit louder, a bit colder.

He did not know what to say. She had lied to him. He reached for cigarettes and matches, felt the fire warming his lips.

She sighed. "And you might as well know the rest. There wasn't even a friend. I just didn't want you to walk with me . . . and then I . . . didn't want . . . to lose you." She had begun to cry; she was gasping. Finally: "You understand how I can hurt you? I don't mean to—really. I just . . . I just . . ."

He crushed out his cigarette and knit his fingers, wondering how many more times, and about what, she had lied to him. He wondered whether he could trust her, whether he still loved her. For a moment he felt nothing for her, could have walked from the apartment and into the street as he had done with Etta-Sue. But then that moment passed gently by and he began to think why she had told him such lies: because she loved him and did not want to lose him. She did love him. He was certain. And he loved her. He was certain of that too. And if they loved each other they could be happy, and she would not have to lie. "Come here, Ragan."

She came slowly across the room toward him, stopped a few feet away, then came closer. He raised his arms to her. Her hands rested on his shoulders, then she knelt in front of him and slipped her arms around his neck. "I'm sor—"

His hands moved across her back, across the slick nylon of her blouse, over the elastic, ribs, and snap of her bra. He let his hand rest there. "Marry me, Ragan. It'll be good."

She let him go, pushed back until he could feel her breath on his face. "You have to let me think. I have to be alone. I want to be sure I'm doing the right thing for us and when you're around I can't think clearly."

He nodded. "I'll leave you here. I got to go downtown any-way." This was true. He had to make final arrangements for a date for both him and Hardie, their groups alternating sets. He could have done it by phone, but he would do it in person.

He kissed her cheek and stood up. "I'll come back around seven and we'll go to dinner or something. All right?"

"Call first, all right?" She was anxious. "Call, so I'll know when you're coming. Call at eight."

"All right, Ragan." He did not like the idea, but agreed, not wanting to upset the delicate balance of her feelings.

He finished his business quickly—they would open the next night—and, having a few hours, went up to a winter-saddened Harlem. His skin burned with the damp wind; his ungloved cane-hand was numb. He stopped in several bars, making his way through murmuring early evening knots of people, through the steamy mixture of beer, perfume and sweat. He asked the time constantly. Finally, at seven minutes to eight, unable to wait any longer, he took down the receiver of a boothless phone, deposited his money, and with his thumb anchored on zero, dialed their number. The phone buzzed twice.

"Hello?" He did not recognize the voice, and was about to hang up. "Ludlow?" It was the voice of a white woman from New York.

He covered his other ear. "Yes. Where's Ragan?" She must have had a friend come to sit with her.

"Do you remember me?" There was a crackling pause. "You met me, I guess, the same night you met Ragan. Remember?"

"Sure. Look, where's Ragan? Can I speak to her?"

"I'm sorry, Ludlow."

"You didn't do nothing. Let me talk to Ragan." He was angry. He may have already realized what had happened, may have been hiding behind his rage to avoid the pain of it.

"She's gone."

"Put her on."

"I can't tell you where. But she'll—"

"What you mean you can't tell me? Put her on, will you?"

"She's gone. But she'll get in touch with you."

"Look, where'd she go?"

"I'm sorry, Ludlow." She paused. He was putting the receiver on the hook, when she squawked, a long way from his ear now, "Nice talking to you again, Ludlow."

He rushed into the street and asked the first person he met to get him a cab. When he arrived home, even Ragan's friend was gone.

7

For the past five days a headache had been stalking, circling him. He had waited for Ragan's call, sitting in their apartment, the smell of their life together still painfully strong in the rooms. When it came time to go to work, he did so reluctantly, certain she would call the apartment while he was out. He realized finally she could just as well call him at work, while he was playing. To make himself easy to find when he was not on the stand, he always sat in a small room, near the kitchen, where the musicians hung their coats.

"It shouldn't be long now." He spoke aloud, though he was alone. "She'll get her mind straight soon now." He could feel his clothes, every part of his body where material scraped his flesh. At times, he could even feel the individual threads. Around his ears, the crinkly hair felt like tiny shocks.

Women wore their clothes far tighter than men—underpants, bras, garter belts and stockings. He wondered if they could feel their clothes. Probably not. Usually he could not even feel his own. He wondered if Ragan, about to pick up the telephone to call him, could feel her clothes. Malveen, a long time ago, must have felt hers. When he had removed her bra, it had left designs on her breasts, small grooves and bumps.

Ragan had nicer breasts than Malveen, or than Etta-Sue. Ragan's breasts were not as big as either of theirs, but they fit his hand perfectly.

That baby might have breasts now. If he remembered correctly she would be eleven next month. Girls of fifteen sometimes had large, well-developed breasts. Perhaps an eleven-year-old girl would have at least hard, tiny breasts.

Outside, applause boiled over the end of Hardie's number. After a moment the trombone player started another song. Ludlow listened for a while, trying to decide if he would go outside and take a table. "No." Hardie was good, and so was his bassist, but his drummer played too loud and his pianist made too many mistakes.

Perhaps he and Hardie could form a new group. But then he would not know what to do with Reno. Ludlow sounded good with either Reno's tenor or Hardie's trombone, but together, the three of them would sound like a sweet society dance band.

His buttocks were numb, his feet cold, his elbow sore; he had been too long in one position. He shifted, concentrating on the pain in his elbow, then laughed out loud, drowning out Hardie's playing. "Got to be careful for my elbows. Somebody's all the time grabbing me by one!" He got up and opened the door to let in Hardie's solo. Hardie could play the saddest ballad and he would make it happy. That was because Hardie was happy, living in the Bronx, his garden smelling of lilac and roses.

His elbow was still sore and he rubbed it. "Without my God damn elbows, I wouldn'ta even played with Inez." His first day in New York, a stranger, a Negro had taken him by the elbow, asked him where he was going, and had volunteered to guide him to the theater in Harlem where Inez Cunningham was working.

Ludlow's head was out of the door. To his left, the crashing pots and pans, the clatter of dishes in a steel tub, the jangle of silverware, the screaming waiters distracted him. Guiding himself along the wall, he went toward the kitchen, away from the music, pushed through the smooth-swinging door.

The crash of dishes seemed to be all around him. "Hey, you clumsy bastard!" A voice came from the floor.

Ludlow was already yelling. "Keep quiet out here, will you!"

Silence pressed against his skin, and then, far off, water gushed. For an instant, he shivered beneath a waterfall.

"Clumsy blind bastard. I got to pay for breakage, you know." It was only a whisper, from the floor, just above the rattle of dishes.

"What? Shut up!" Trying to kick out at the voice, he pulled himself off balance, but did not fall down.

There was some laughter, then grumbling. Footsteps shuffled closer, like the first day at the Home.

Afraid, he stumbled toward the door, pushed through into the hall. When the wall ended, he turned into the open door of the coatroom and slammed it behind him. He sat down and concentrated on Hardie. The tone was so full that he imagined himself to be in the very bell of the trombone, the brass ringing and shaking around him. Perhaps he would tell Hardie about Ragan; perhaps Hardie could reach her and tell her to call.

He was thirsty and wanted to go into the kitchen for a glass of water, but the waiters and cooks would probably not give it to him. He could go to the bar and get a drink; they liked him at the bar. He got up and opened the door, stepped forward, and bumped into someone. "Where you going?—Hey, you don't look too good." It was Reno.

Ignoring the comment, he answered the question. "Getting a drink." He was not certain he wanted it now. He suddenly craved honey and hard, foreign bread. It would taste like a honeycomb. Once he and Ragan had driven into the country and bought honeycomb. He did not want to think about it. "How long until we play?"

"Fifteen minutes. Hey, look, you feel sick? Maybe you should—"

"Mind your own God damn business, will you?" His right hand, knotted into a fist, moved toward Reno's voice. He tried to stop it, but could not. He missed, his fist dragging him to the opposite wall.

"What's wrong with you, Ludlow?"

His head and stomach seemed to be connected, pain flowing between them. He stumbled toward Reno. "I'm sorry, man. Really. You're my boy. You know that, don't you?"

"Sure, Ludlow. Hey, what's the trouble?" Reno was confused.

Perhaps Reno, who had gone to college, would know why Ragan had left. But Ludlow did not have the courage to tell him she was gone, and disguised the question. "Listen, I want to ask you something important."

"Go on." Reno was suspicious.

"You went to college, right? So what you think white folks want from us?"

"You serious?"

"Yeah, I'm serious."

Reno began slowly, expecting some kind of joke. "They want us to be what they think we are." He paused. "Now what that is depends on the particular white man you dealing with. You still with me?"

"Yeah. Yeah." The boy was making sense.

"Most of them want to think we're not dangerous. And that means they don't want us to be human. Because if I learned anything at all in college, it's that everybody's just naturally dangerous." He was embarrassed. "All right?"

Ludlow nodded. Reno had just given him the answer. He knew why Ragan had left, knew what he had to do to make her come back. "I don't feel good, man. I need some air. Could you get me to the door?"

"Sure, but don't you think—"

"Get me to the door, will you please?"

Reno took his elbow, guided him down the hall and into the club. Hardie was soloing now, building, playing an uptempo blues. He thought about how Hardie had always made white people think he was not at all dangerous. That was why they permitted Hardie to be happy.

They came to the foot of the stairs leading to the street. "Can you make it alone?"

Ludlow nodded. "Do me a favor? Wait here to take me back. I'll only be five minutes?"

"Sure you don't want me to go with you?"

"No. Things to think about." He started up the steps, pushed through the door into the cold wind. His nose began to run, his neck was cold. He had forgotten his overcoat. His cane seemed an icicle. He went to his right, reached the corner and went right again. It should be close by now. He put his hand against cold glass, felt his way into a doorway and opened a door. "This a magic store?"

The clerk's answer came from behind a radio which played popular violin music. "Yeah?"

Ludlow closed the door. "You got make-up?"

The clerk was angry and rushing toward him. "I don't want you God damn queens in here!"

Ludlow raised his cane hand. "I mean stage make-up, like they use in minstrel shows. Blackface." Once, while still with Inez Cunningham, they had appeared on the same bill as a minstrel show. Standing in the wings, he had listened to the cruel jokes, the slurred speech of white men imitating Negroes. "Blackface. That stuff?"

The clerk was bewildered now. "What're you—kidding or something?" This must have been part of it too. Some would pretend they did not understand what Ludlow had to do.

"You got it?"

"I don't mean no offense, buddy, but . . . you don't need nothing like that."

"You got the make-up?"

"Sure. I didn't mean nothing." He circled the counter. A drawer slid open and tins rattled. Then he returned. "This what we got. It's black as—sin." He laughed nervously. "No offense meant."

Ludlow did not have much time. "How much?"

The clerk told him the price. "What's this—some kind of practical joke?"

Ludlow tossed the money on the glass counter, put the tin of make-up into his pocket, and made his way back to the night club.

"You shoulda worn a coat, Ludlow." Reno was concerned.

"Get me to the room, will you?"

"What's wrong with you?" They moved through the crowded club.

"Nothing. How much time we got now?"

"Hardie just started his last number."

When they reached the head of the hall, Ludlow shook free. "I got to do something in there." He pointed down the hall. "Don't come in, all right? And don't let nobody else come in."

"Sure, Ludlow, but—" Reno stopped when he started down the hallway. Perhaps Ludlow should have been less abrupt. He did not want Reno to worry. Then he might try to stop him, ruining Ludlow's plan.

He went into the room and locked the door. He had to get ready. Sitting down, he took the tin of make-up from his pocket and twisted it open and spread it onto his face. It felt like cold hair pomade and smelled like a woman's powder. When he had finished, he stood up and pressed his ear against the door, listening to the last few choruses of Hardie's number. Applause followed and then Hardie spoke, his voice made deeper and more fuzzy by the microphone:

"Thank you, folks. I want you to sit by because in about two minutes we'll have a giant for you, the man who started it all by his-self, Ludlow Washington." There was applause. "All right. So stick around now, hear? Thank you."

Ludlow moved away from the door, shaking his head. He had never been able to speak to an audience like that, so very friendly.

In the hall, they were whispering. Then they began to knock. "Hey, Ludlow? It's Hardie. Ludlow?"

They would try to stop him; he had to keep them away. They did not know how important this was to him. "Hardie? Who else's out there?"

"Just me and Reno. You all right?" And then, almost slyly, "Why don't you open the door?"

"Hardie? I got a gun. I'm planning to kill myself." He hoped they believed him. Reno might think he had bought it while he was outside.

Beyond the door for a moment, there was only the murmuring, glass-clicking audience. Then Hardie again: "Awh, man. What you want to do that for?"

"You don't want me to?" He hated doing all this, using Hardie, and what he would have to do in a few moments.

"No, man. You got to stay alive. . . . How the hell will I know what to play if I can't copy off you?"

"I got this gun in my left pocket and I can shoot a hole in my stomach if anybody gets near me." He found the make-up tin and put it into his left pocket, gripping it tightly. "All I want really is to go outside on stage and play. That's all. I ain't planning to hurt nobody. You let me do that?"

Hardie whispered to Reno. Then: "Yeah, man. All right."

"Don't try nothing, Hardie."

"All right, man."

He opened the door. "Hello. I won't hurt nobody."

They did not answer; they must be staring at his face. From inside, Ludlow pulled his coat pocket up toward his stomach, and started down the hall. They followed him. "Don't jump me. I won't look good with a hole in my stomach."

They went into the club and Ludlow climbed the stairs. At the same time that he felt the hot lights, the audience applauded. He bowed. He went straight to the microphone. "Thank you, ladies and gentlemen." He stopped, trying to think of words. There was deep laughter from the back of the room, then several snickers. They had noticed the make-up. Ludlow hunched his shoulders, stuck out his lips, grinned, bowed several more times.

He began to sweat; his head was throbbing steadily now and he had trouble remembering what he planned to do. "Ain't out here to play music tonight, folks. No sir!" He tried to make himself sound as ignorant as he could. He was imitating the minstrels. "Going to tell you folks some funny stories and sing some songs." He waited for laughter; there was less now. "You understand now? Good. You see, I ain't dangerous. Honest!" Such pleas were against the rules, he knew. He was supposed only to perform. On that basis alone, they would decide if he was dangerous.

He felt Hardie at his shoulder, whispering. "Come on, man. Don't make no ass of yourself in front of these white people."

Ludlow put his right hand over the microphone. "That's the point. It's the only way I can get Ragan back, man." He turned to the audience again. "Excuse me, folks. Trouble with one of the field niggers." He laughed. A few joined him, but nervously; he could not understand that.

"Heard a good joke the other day. Maybe you'd like it. It seems like Sam, the nigger roustabout in a small circus down South, got paid fifty dollars to screw Gertrude, the gorilla, who was the big attraction in the circus. Gertrude was only happy when she was getting screwed, and people only come to the circus when Gertrude was happy. So the first time Sam screwed her, they chained Gertrude down and put a muzzle on her so Sam wouldn't get all bit up. They also had canvas on the cage so wouldn't nobody see Sam doing it. That was to save Sam's pride. So Sam went into the cage and climbed right on her. After a while, the men standing around the cage, they hear Sam screaming and yelling. They rush inside thinking maybe Sam's in danger. But when they get in there, Sam turns around, pumping away, puffing and blowing, and says, 'This is the best fuck I ever had! Take off her muzzle! I want to tongue this sweet thing!'" He laughed to help them along, then stopped. The room was silent. He had not fooled them.

There was a tightness in his throat and the back of his jaws were knotted. His brain broke loose from his skull, banged against the top of his head. Then he felt tears tickling his cheeks, tasted the make-up mixed with the tears. He gripped the microphone with his right hand, his left still in his pocket. "Please! Please! I tried. I ain't dangerous. I'm blind. How could I be dangerous? Can't she come back now? Please send her back. . . ."

As soon as his left hand touched the cold stem of the microphone, Hardie grabbed his arms and pinned them behind his back. Ludlow could no longer stand up, collapsed onto his knees, still begging. Hardie, breathing heavily on his neck, kept a good grip on Ludlow's arms.

Later, they told him he had cried for three days.

PART SIX

INTERVIEW . . .

    I ain't at all ashamed of it. I cracked up. In fact, I cracked up a couple times. But that's about all I really know. One of the doctors tried to tell me what went bad, but I couldn't follow him. Anyway, it didn't matter to me, just as long as I wasn't running around hurting nobody. . . . So when I got out the last time, I was an old man, thirty-four God damn years old, but I'd go into a club and some kid musician'd say, "He Ludlow Washington. He was in on the start, but he couldn't keep up." Hell, I'd been thinking about a lot of things in the hospitals, and I'd been practicing. I was still out front. Only nobody knew it yet. Anyway, I couldn't get much work. No one'd hire any group I'd got together. They was all afraid I'd put on another minstrel show.

I

Another Christmas.

He could not even remember the first five Christmases of his life. The next eleven had been at the Home; on the first one he may have cried the entire day. The remaining were undistinguished, except for the fourth; his master had given him a present. He had never understood why. His first Christmas out of the Home, he was living at Missus Scott's and was still single. He and Hardie had worked, gotten drunk, found two girls. By the next Christmas, he was married, but Etta-Sue was already pregnant. The next three were with Inez Cunningham. The first of those had been the best; he had been eighteen years old, up North for only six months, playing with the best singer in the country. Inez always arranged her bookings to spend Christmas in New York. That first year, after the show, she had taken the group for drinks. She never did it again. Five band Christmases followed —hot dogs instead of turkey, in the back seats of cars or buses. The Christmas after the war ended he had spent with Hardie,

Juanita and Otie. The next was Ragan's Christmas, though he had been traveling. It had not mattered much; he had been in love. There had been seven since Ragan's Christmas, some in, some out of the hospital.

Somewhere down the hall a radio was playing a loud, commercial Christmas song. Footsteps passed his door, humming. He rolled onto his side and went through his Christmases once more. He shook his head, his hair crackling against the pillow. None of them had been very good. Then he laughed. "Hell, why you lying here feeling sorry for yourself?" He pushed down the covers and sat up. The radiator was popping and hissing.

When he finished dressing, had made his bed, he left the hotel and walked a half block to a small diner. The cooks were Chinese, but they prepared the best collard greens and black-eyed peas he had eaten since he left the South. Besides, it was cheap, and, not working very often now, he had to make his money last.

After he had eaten, he took a short walk to listen to Harlem on Christmas. From time to time, when the wind died, the sun was warm on his face. It was quiet; the parties and toasting had all been the night before. Today people stayed home and slept. In the late afternoon he thought he might walk up to a dance hall and find out if the band had any empty chair. After an hour of walking, he went back to his hotel to practice.

Hardie had been waiting for him in the lobby. "How you been, Ludlow?" He was nervous, embarrassed.

"Can't complain, I guess." He thought, then added, "Don't do no good."

Hardie laughed politely. They did not meet very often now. Hardie was doing too well, Ludlow too badly. Hardie felt guilty about this and, to spare him anguish, Ludlow turned down Hardie's dinner invitations, ignored his phone calls. He still liked Hardie a great deal.

They went to Ludlow's room and sat down. On the bed, Ludlow smiled, trying to put Hardie at ease. "How's everybody?" Besides Otie, Hardie now had a little girl.

"Fine, fine. Girl's in school now. Smart." His chair squeaked. "Ludlow . . . I feel funny coming down here . . . well, look, I got some work for you."

Ludlow did not answer. He would not turn it down, whatever it was, but the less gratitude he displayed the better.

"I don't like doing you favors, but I know you need all the work you can get. How things been—really?"

Ludlow told the truth. "You know, man. Little dances, rock bands, a couple records. But I'm living and I'm out." Hardie and Juanita had been the only people to visit him the several times he had been in the hospital.

"Well, this is pretty good. You know about the concert?"

Ludlow nodded. That evening there was a big jazz concert downtown.

"All I got you was a spot in the jam session. But you oughta get fifty. I wish—" He slapped his thigh. "I wish you had a group and could show them what it's about. Remember that night—" He faltered, went on: "Remember I said you couldn't die because then I wouldn't know what to play?"

Ludlow nodded. He had gone over that night many times with the doctors.

"It was true. It always been true and it'll be true for the next twenty years. It true for me and anybody else playing today."

"What time should I get there tonight?"

"Eight oughta be all right. I don't know how many numbers you'll play, but the fifty's good, don't you think?"

Ludlow sighed. "Listen, Hardie, you ain't got to feel bad because you making money and I ain't. You deserve to make money. You understand me?"

Hardie was silent for a full minute, probably recovering from his surprise. "I don't deserve it more than you do."

"Yes, you do. That's what I want you to understand." He took a deep breath. "I don't know what it was—not having no family, or not having no eyes, or something else—but I didn't grow up learning all the things I should. I mean, the blind home taught me how to eat my food and cross the street, but they left out some things. Maybe it was just that the teachers didn't know, or even that they knew it but didn't want to teach it. Or maybe it was just me. But you know what it taken me all this time to learn? To know what people to trust. And if you think that ain't important for a blind Negro to know, you crazy." He paused. "Remember what you told me before I married Etta-Sue?"

"Man, that was a long—"

"I do. You told me to make sure the girl was with me. I made the same God damn mistake two times. Two times! Well, I don't need no more lessons." He paused. "How many girls you went with before you married Juanita?"

Hardie answered with a laugh.

"How come you knew to pick the right one outa that mob?"

"I never did expect to get married. I figured all women for con artists."

Ludlow nodded. "Yeah. And I always wanted to get married, to have a family and somebody to care about me. Why?" He smiled. "Go ask my doctors. They got files on the shit in my head." He laughed, put his hands on his knees and stood up. "You got to go now. I want to practice."

Hardie took a deep breath. "Listen, Ludlow, why don't you ride up home and have dinner?"

"It's your Christmas, man." He shook his head. "It ain't mine." He smiled. "But thanks anyways." He went to the door and opened it.

Hardie sighed and got up, coming to Ludlow's side. "I'll see you tonight."

He closed the door, went to the dresser and put together his instrument. In the bell was a dent and the finish was grainy. Before he began his warm-up scales he thought again about the things he had said to Hardie and smiled. They had sounded as good in the air as they had in his head.

That evening after the concert, as he waited backstage for Hardie, who was going to drive him uptown, a girl introduced herself as Harriet Lewis and asked if she could interview him for her college newspaper. Surprised and a little flattered that someone, even a college girl, should still want to interview him, he submitted to her questioning. It was five minutes before he realized she was a Negro, and then it was not her accent (Midwestern and faintly Jewish) which told him, but instead her knowledge of the Southside of Chicago. After that he attempted to answer her too-serious questions much more seriously—and to ask some questions himself. He found out she was twenty-one and decided that she probably had more problems than he wanted to bother with, even though it would have been nice to make love to someone on Christmas. They talked ten minutes more, until Hardie came for him, and when she had finished questioning him about his creative processes and the true nature of improvisation, she took his address and promised to send him a copy of her article.

Ludlow and Hardie did not speak until they left the northern end of the park. "That little girl is how old? Seventeen?"

"You ever hear from Etta-Sue, Ludlow?" Hardie had known he was thinking about New Marsails.

Ludlow shook his head. "Why should I?"

"No reason."

"Sometimes I do wonder what the little girl is doing. Sometimes I almost send her a card or a present. Then I say—hell, you dropped that behind you, and ain't no running back to pick it up."

Sometimes too he wondered what had happened to Ragan, where she had gone, whether or not she had actually given birth to a child, what it had been and what she had done with it. He wondered if she had married, and what kind of man her husband might be. In the beginning, it had been painful to think about Ragan because he had still loved her. Finally he had not loved her any more and could not even understand how he had ever loved her at all. Now this was what puzzled him most. He knew if ever he understood why he had fallen in love with Ragan, he would have discovered something important about himself.

Hardie made a turn and stopped. "Ludlow? . . ."

"Forget it, man. It ain't Christmas every day. They all ain't this bad." He laughed, noticing a bitter edge to it, and left the car quickly.

That night, hating himself as he did it, he dictated, to a sleepy and slightly drunk desk clerk, a short note to his daughter. The day after Christmas he woke up and dressed early enough to retrieve and destroy it before it had been mailed.

2

One afternoon a month later, Miss Harriet Lewis knocked at his door, interrupting his practice. Instead of asking her inside, he put on his coat and took her to his diner for a cup of coffee. Walking beside her, he wondered why he had not wanted to be alone with her.

They sat at the end of the counter nearest the kitchen and she read what she had written about him. It was strange to listen to his words being spoken by someone else. When she finished, she asked him if he approved.

"I really sound like that?"

"I hope so." She paused, then asked, "How've you been?"

He remembered she had asked this earlier. "All right." He sipped his coffee. In the kitchen, the cooks argued in Chinese, more like singing than shouting.

"I didn't interrupt you, did I?" She sounded guilty.

"From what?"

"Practicing."

He shook his head. "I was almost finished." One of the Chinese had stomped by them, heading down the counter. The other screamed after him.

"How you been since Christmas?" He could not understand why he found it so hard to talk to her.

"I've been studying for my finals."

He smiled. "They on the creative process? You sure that don't got nothing to do with hair?"

"No." She laughed at the joke. "I think maybe I should've mailed you the article." Her voice was flat.

"Why?" He knew the answer already.

"Because you obviously don't want to be bothered with me." She was not angry; she had stated a fact.

"It ain't that, Miss Lewis. I just don't know what the hell to say to you. It been a long time since I was twenty-one—and I ain't never been to college."

"Oh."

He could tell nothing from the one word. "You know I got a girl, a daughter almost your age—seventeen?"

"Oh?" He knew she was merely pretending interest. "Where is she?"

He shrugged. "Probably down South. I left her mama when she was a baby." He wondered why he had blurted this. He waited for her reply, but there was none. "Your tests, they hard?"

"Do you want me to go back to school now?"

He was surprised to discover he could not answer.

"Can you get back to your hotel?"

"Listen, Miss Lewis—"

Suddenly she was very angry. "I know very well how old you are—exactly thirty-five years, ten months! So I don't have to be warned."

"All right, Miss Lewis. I was—"

"And I'm not begging you to sleep with me either. So what are you frightened of?"

"All right, Miss Lewis." He put down his cup.

"And for Christ's sake, don't call me Miss Lewis!" She turned away. "Can I have another cup of coffee please?" She was speaking to one of the Chinese, who a moment later slid the saucer across the counter.

For what seemed like a long while they sat in silence, the cooks squabbling behind the counter. At first Ludlow tried in vain to think of something to say to her. Finally he decided he would say nothing at all. He had enough problems without getting involved with a twenty-one-year-old college girl.

Her cup clinked into its saucer one last time and she got up, rustled into her overcoat, opened and snapped her purse. "I have to catch a train."

He tilted his head. "Thanks for bringing the newspaper."

"I better catch my train." Then before he realized she was not moving away, a clear, clean scent came close and a kiss popped lightly on his cheek. Her heels faded into the shouting of the Chinese, who was at the other end of the counter.

Ludlow shook his head, wondering why the wrong girls always fell in love with him.

3

She returned two days later, a Saturday, saying that she had been in the neighborhood visiting her uncle, had dropped by simply to say hello. He was suspicious of her, but she seemed so calm, so relaxed that he soon put aside his suspicions. She sat in a chair in his hotel room talking about her schoolwork as if he were interested. Just as he was relaxing, she got up and left.

The following Friday she knocked at his door again. She had been given two tickets to a concert of West African music, and she had thought he might want to go. He was not working that evening; they ate at his diner, and went to the concert. Afterward she brought him to his hotel, shook his hand and hailed a taxi.

Not long after that he was afflicted with some kind of stomach ailment which made him vomit, gave him diarrhea and kept him in bed for several days. As if she somehow knew or had even poisoned his system herself, she happened to be visiting her uncle and dropped by. Finding him sick, she was out of his room and back in a matter of minutes with medicine and magazines, which she read aloud to him the entire afternoon.

In the next two months she visited too often for him to think her visits were at all coincidental. But he did not know how to stop her. Somehow he sensed that if he told her not to come, she would agree, but that a few days later she would be knocking on his door, apologizing for bothering him and giving some good excuse for being there. The only thing for him to do would be to remain cold and distant until her infatuation subsided. This he did, but it did not work. She seemed not at all disheartened; if anything, she was more buoyant than ever.

Finally, one day just as spring was taking full possession of the air, and she had visited him, happening to have been to a dentist in the neighborhood, he decided to end the game.

They had stopped in an air-conditioned bar for beer. He sipped his, the foam tickling his upper lip, then put it down. "Okay. How come you doing all this?"

"All what?" She had been humming with the jukebox.

"How come all this visiting?"

"Don't you know?"

"No." He may have, but wanted her to say it.

She sipped her beer. "I decided to be in love with you. What about you?"

"No, ma'am! I don't love you. I don't even want to love you."

"All right. Can I have another beer?"

He reached out, found and gripped her arm. "What you want from me?" And then, before she could even answer: "I ain't got nothing for you."

"That doesn't matter, though it'd be very nice if you loved me. But it doesn't matter. I have something to give you."

He let go her arm. "But why me?"

218

"You're the only man I feel like loving at the moment."

His face must have shown that he was bewildered by her. She went on: "Four years ago, when I came east to college, I was pretty sure I'd go back home this June and marry some dentist my parents'd picked out for me. You know, dentists are very big in the middle class this year—they make such a steady income. But when I got here, I met a few of those potential dentists, and now, if I know anything, it's that I don't want to marry some respectable little colored boy who went to an Ivy League school and hopes if he makes straight A's and enough money pulling teeth, his skin'll be white one morning when he wakes up." She stopped, laughed. "But I don't think it's a good idea for a girl to go around not loving anyone at all. It gets her out of practice." She sighed. "So when I met you last Christmas, I thought about it for a month and then decided I'd love you since you obviously need to be loved by someone."

"You serious?"

"Oh, I'm serious all right. Can't you tell?"

"What you mean by love? Like a mother, a sister or a wife?"

"A wife."

He was certain she was fooling, or bragging, or making promises she would not keep. He could not resist challenging her. "What'd you say if I said to you—Wife, let's run back to the hotel and knock off a piece?"

"Yes. But after I have another beer."

He still did not believe her. "You're on, baby. Get your beer."

She ordered, and, talking happily to him about a variety of things, drank the beer. Then she said she was ready and they went out into the noisy Harlem springtime.

Behind locked doors, he listened to her undress. Then she went to the bed; the springs whined and crackled under her.

Still surprised, and knowing she must be watching him, he undressed, climbed into bed beside her and put his arms around her, finding her skin cool even in the warm room. She did not wear perfume, only lots of powder, and her skin was slippery. On her back were many bumps the size of the heads of pins. There was a hook-shaped scar, the length of his thumb, on her right buttock. He asked about it; she had arthritis at one time, she said.

He gave her a last chance to back out—and, he realized, himself too. "You sure you ain't just all talk?"

She hesitated. "I don't think so."

"Okay." He kissed her, and enjoyed it. "I believe you."

4

It was good having a steady woman again—especially since Harriet demanded nothing of him. He knew he could break it off at any time. He had made no promises. He did not love Harriet, but he certainly liked her a great deal and showed her that he did. He paid attention when she complained about some injustice at school, listened and soothed her when she cried because she was gaining weight or when her face started to break out. At first he thought little of these attentions, but he came to realize they were quite important, not only to her, but to himself. He realized he had never before paid so much unselfish attention to anyone. Perhaps Etta-Sue and Ragan had not betrayed him as much as he had betrayed himself by not really listening to them. Perhaps if he had listened to them, really examined their words, they would never have disillusioned and betrayed him, because perhaps he would never have trusted or had any illusions about them.

On the same day that Harriet graduated from college, Ludlow

was offered a job in a quartet that played at a small Negro resort hotel an hour's drive from the city. Harriet went along, securing a job as a waitress in the dining room.

She worked most of the day, and just when she was finishing, his hours were beginning. Sometimes she would come to listen to him, but most often she slept, getting up when he was finished. In the cricket-filled nights they would sit on the damp grass behind the hotel, or walk to the small pond where the guests swam. Sometimes Harriet would undress and swim, while he sat on the cold sand beside her still-warm clothes. Ludlow never went into the water; he could not swim.

There were two sounds to her swimming: the dull, low bubbling of her kick and the higher splash of her arms. His hands squeezed the damp sand into a ball.

She ran toward him, the water crackling. "You're sweating. Why don't you come in?"

She was standing close over him, giving off cold. He laughed. "Don't want me around no more, huh? Well, you don't have to drown me. I'll just go."

She squatted in front of him. Cold lips kissed his. "I won't let you drown, Ludlow. I promise."

He tried to remember the last time he had been in the water, could not. He shook his head, vaguely afraid. "We ain't got no towel."

"Yes, we do. I brought one tonight. I can teach you to swim. I'm an instructor in the Red Cross." She was proud of that.

"That so?" He pretended to be impressed.

"I worked very hard. I had to tow a man a hundred yards."

"What man?"

"Jealous?" She wanted him to be.

He shook his head. "I didn't know you then."

222

"Won't you come swimming?"

She seemed so disappointed that for an instant he weakened. "Sure." He stood up and took off his jacket and unbuckled his belt. Once again he was afraid, as if there were something waiting for him in the water.

When he was undressed, a breeze blowing cool on his warm skin, she took his hand and led him slowly into the water. It rose over his shins and knees, up his thighs, painful and refreshing. Then it was a knife between his legs. . . .

His teeth were chattering; his brother gripped his hand tighter. "He scared, Papa." His brother shouted toward the shore, a mile away.

"Don't be scared, Luddy." His father's voice came across the water, riding small waves. "He'll hold you. Don't worry."

"He still shaking." His brother's voice tickled his ear: "Don't shake, Luddy. I'll keep you all right."

His teeth clicked rapidly. He was moaning. He tried to tell his brother he was not afraid, but could not speak.

"He shaking like mad, Papa."

"You bring him in here then." His mother did not shout, but her voice came clearly on the small waves of the pond. "He'll learn to swim tomorrow."

"Come on, Luddy, you don't got to shake no more." His brother took his shoulders and turned him around. The water slid down his legs. Then the sand was warm and dry. The heat came from high up, through a breeze. "He still shaking, Mama. He crying too." His brother disapproved.

"Bring him here." His mother was sitting on the sand, her voice level with his ears.

His brother led him to her and then her hands took his waist, and pulled him gently to her, into her lap. For a moment, she released him with one hand, fiddled with something above his head. Her skin tasted of salt; his face brushed soft, warm flesh. Then his lips found the small button of her nipple and he was sucking. "Don't cry now, Luddy." Her voice came down to his ear, and through her breast too. "Mama'll take care of you. Don't cry."

"He all right?" His father was close too, his breath smelling of the beer he had been drinking.

"He'll be all right soon." When her voice stopped, over the sound of waves on the shore, his brother paddled away in the water. . . .

"Ludlow, don't cry." Harriet had stopped pulling him, had dropped his hand, put her arms around his waist, and kissed him.

"God damn mother-fucker!" He was too ashamed to say anything else. "Damn mother-fucking bastard!"

"It's all right. Come on. It's all right. I'll take you out. Come on." She pulled him into ankle-deep water. They stood on wet sand; the water covering their feet was warmer than the air. "It's all right."

"Shit!" He stopped, sighed and told her what had happened to him, embarrassed, ashamed and confused to be remembering such things and, worse, to cry over them. When he had finished, she only kissed him and told him she loved him.

He lowered and shook his head as he had often done when she told him this.

She shrugged, a smile in her voice. "It doesn't matter."

They dried off, put on their clothes, then sat down on the sand, and Ludlow talked. He could not stop himself. He told her everything, about Etta-Sue and Ragan and how he thought sometimes about the daughter he knew he had, and the child he was not certain had ever been born. He wondered how much of what had happened to him was his fault, or someone else's fault, or perhaps no one's fault at all. He told Harriet he might never love her, and again she replied that she had decided to love him and that would be enough for a while.

The coming day began to dry the air; Harriet told him it was time for her to set the tables in the dining room. They walked toward the hotel, his hand on her elbow.

"Don't you want to get married and have kids and all that?" This still bothered him. He had never met anyone who seemed to want nothing.

"Sure." She paused. "But I have time."

"Well, don't get too tied up here now." He smiled.

"I told you that's my problem." She sounded slightly angry.

"All right."

"You just remember it."

They went on to the row of cabins where the help and the musicians stayed. They had been assigned to different cabins, but they had worked out an arrangement with their cabin mates so they could stay together. Ludlow stood on the second step. "You'll be dragging all day." He put his hand on top of her damp head.

"I'll sleep this afternoon." She grew very serious. "Are you all right?"

He nodded. "I'm doing fine." He realized then, his hand in her damp, curly hair, how very much he liked her.

5

He waited for Harriet in a clearing in the woods. They had found it one afternoon, a treeless square twenty paces long, fifteen paces wide. He had come there alone, his instrument case in his hand, his feet knowing he was straying off the path when his footfalls were softened by leaves and pine needles. He sat now, birds and leaves singing and shuffling overhead, and practiced. Harriet had gone into the city for the day, but would return soon.

Sitting on a rough log in the late summer afternoon, he had been thinking how much he hated winter. Nothing good had ever happened to him in the winter, and most of the bad. He could not remember ever having been happy when he was cold.

Perhaps he and Harriet would go South—not to New Marsails of course; he did not want to meet Etta-Sue or his daughter and upset their lives. But he and Harriet could find some place warm and he could play with a small group and make enough to live. He smiled at the idea, sadness tugging him downward; he would never do such a thing. He was certain, but did not know why.

He wondered what time it was. It seemed as if an evening breeze, cooler, was blowing down the well formed by the trees. He began to play again, drowning out the sounds of the clearing.

The leaves on the path began to rattle steadily, the hissing of small, dry beads in a gourd. He stopped playing. Under the hissing came the thump of her running steps. "Hiya, baby."

"I have the greatest thing—"

"I know you do. Have a good day?" He bent forward, opened his case and put down his instrument. "Come here and tell me." He opened his arms; she sat on his lap.

"A wonderful day!" She put her arms around his neck, squeezed him tight and kissed him. He began to want to make love to her, but she was also beginning to get heavy. He could feel the rough bark through his pants.

"Listen to me, Ludlow."

He put his hand on her side and tickled her, then kissed her again. "I missed you, girl."

"I missed you too, Ludlow." She stopped laughing. "But listen."

"Okay, but you getting heavy; move off!" He patted her behind.

She got up, then sat on the ground between his knees, her back to him. "Now listen to me. This is really important." She meant it. He did not reply. "I bought *Four-Four* today because I thought you'd like to know who was doing what in New York and stuff like that. And I was reading it myself coming back here and there's an article about you, Ludlow." She stopped, probably waiting for an answer. But she had not told him enough.

"Don't you understand? It's all over now." She moved forward

227

and then she had turned around to face him, her hands on his knees. "All the bad times are over for you."

He smiled; she was so earnest. "How you know?"

"Because—I'm telling you—there's a big article about you with pictures and everything. Wait a minute." She rummaged through her purse. The teeth of a comb sawed, money jingled. "Okay. It's called 'Why Do We Waste Our Geniuses?' It starts: *As you can see from the title, this will not be simply another review of another record. What I will try to do in the next twelve hundred words, is to right an almost unforgivable wrong, to bring about justice. It all starts with a recording, however, the newly issued album of six sides of the now famous concert of Christmas last.*"

The writer, *Four-Four* magazine's most widely known and respected jazz critic, went on to tell that he had been ill the Christmas before and had been unable to attend the concert. But he was now glad he had not seen it because perhaps, like everyone else he had talked to, he might have walked out after the big-name groups had finished and missed the jam session.

"*Side five was taken up with the jam session. You must all understand the hazards involved in a jam session. Usually there has been no rehearsal and the statement of the theme (if there is a theme) is usually shoddy. The solos are usually below par.*

"*Even so, I listened through a series of good to excellent solos—and then thunder struck! Perhaps 'brave' seems a strange word to describe a tone, but brave it was, and deep and strong. Whoever was playing, and I did not immediately recognize the musician and had not read the album's liner notes, had more than mastered his instrument. A name went through my mind—Ludlow Washington. Yes, this musician sounded a great deal like Ludlow Washington, though, of course, it could not be he. Every-*

one knows that seven or eight years ago Washington went berserk on the stage of a New York night club and was committed to a mental hospital. For all I knew, he was still there, babbling obscenely as he had that winter night so long ago.

"Whoever was playing had learned a great deal from Washington, but that was not the most astounding thing. This musician had not only learned, he had built upon what he had learned. He was better than Ludlow Washington!"

Of course the writer had been listening to no one but Ludlow Washington, and he had decided he would try to find him. He contacted Ludlow's friend, Otis Hardie, who could only give him an address in Harlem.

"So I went to Harlem, to a dingy hotel. The desk clerk told me that Washington had been staying there, but had checked out in June, leaving no forwarding address.

"That was where the trail ended. Disappointed, I returned home and listened to all of Ludlow Washington's records, starting with Inez Cunningham, ending with the concert. The emotion I experienced while listening to these uniformly brilliant performances was one of admiration, respect, gratitude and shame —the last because I realized that I, and all of us who love jazz, had been guilty of a grave crime. We had wasted, neglected, the only undisputed genius jazz has produced in the last two decades; we have allowed him to spend the last seven years in cheap hotels, playing in bad rock-and-roll bands. But our neglect, however bad that may be, is not the worst crime. We have cheated ourselves of the best music we will probably hear in our lifetime. Now you understand the title of this essay: 'Why do we waste our geniuses?'

"And Ludlow Washington, where is he now? Returned once again, without notice, to the wards of the insane, or dying, or

perhaps even dead? I would give a great deal to know the answer to this question. This I do know: If Ludlow Washington is alive, and sane, he is playing—thrilling all those lucky enough to be within hearing.

Harriet finished and sighed. "Isn't that wonderful?"

Ludlow, in reply, began to laugh and could not stop himself until the bones in his head seemed ready to burst, until the muscles in his neck ached. "You seen anybody being thrilled by my playing lately?" He laughed again.

"Ludlow, don't. Don't you realize? You can go back to New York and start a new group and work in places where people actually care about what you play." She took his hand.

She was right. He could return to New York, but for some reason he was not nearly as excited as he would have thought. He supposed he had been waiting for something like this to happen. Perhaps the belief that it would happen had kept him playing.

"Ludlow, you can go back."

He thought of New York as it had been for him seven years before. He remembered himself standing on a stage, under dry heat, playing his best into the face of tinkling glasses, ringing telephones, belling cash registers, screaming waiters, jingling money, booming laughter, and cackling women. Even when he was popular, there had not been much appreciation.

He laughed. "If I want to."

"But of course you do." She was bewildered. "You should be playing in better groups than you're playing in now. People shouldn't be dancing while you play."

The guests at the hotel did dance. But a person had to be listening to dance. If they were dancing, if the scraping of their feet rose to the bandstand, he knew at least he had reached them. Perhaps it was too much to ask of people that they sit for hours and simply listen. But in New York they did not dance, they did not listen. The audience sat and talked, and in a corner, where their music would not bother the audience too much, the musicians played. He remembered what Norman Spencer had told him once about the old Harlem rent parties. "We wasn't making no money then, but hell, man, you knew that the twenty or thirty or fifty folks in that one small, cabbage-smelling room was enjoying what you was doing. You'd lean into the keys, and behind you they was having the best old time ever. Shit, you ask me why I don't go downtown? That's another reason." Ludlow smiled, remembering the pianist's bitter voice. Too bad there were no more rent parties.

"Ludlow?" Harriet was shaking his arms. "Ludlow, don't you want to go back to New York?"

"I don't know."

She released her grip. "Why not? Because of that girl?"

It could be because of Ragan. She was New York too. But perhaps it was not that New York would bring back memories of her, that every time he played there he would remember he had met Ragan there, had broken down there. Perhaps it was that New York had created Ragan, had made her what she was. He was not afraid to go back. He had been there since Ragan left him. But then, perhaps Harlem was not New York at all.

"No. Ain't her. But if I go back and take their money, I got to live like they tell me. You got to be careful who you take money from in this world."

"You can live however you want, Ludlow."

"And that's what I got to decide." He did not want to talk about it any more now, and stood up. "Well, we can't go back for

231

two weeks anyway, not until the season's played out. New York'll just have to wait."

She stood up. "What are—"

"Don't you got to work, sweetie?"

She said Yes, and they walked back to their cabin.

6

He folded the last shirt, closed and pushed in the snaps of the suitcase. Then he sat on the bed to wait for Harriet to return from the manager's office.

The season had ended two days before, with a big party for the dozen or so remaining guests. The day before, one by one, their cars filling the air with exhaust and dry dust, they had left for the city. Harriet had stayed an extra day to help clean and close the rooms, persuading Ludlow they would need the extra day's pay until he could form his new group.

It had been two weeks since she returned from the city with the magazine and the article about Ludlow. Most of the time since, he had been trying to decide what he wanted to do. He had collected and ordered the bits and pieces of his life and he thought he had found a pattern. Sitting now on one of the two beds they had shared during the past eight weeks, pushed apart once again to their original positions on opposite walls, he thought he knew.

Her footsteps knocked on the small porch; the loose doorknob rattled.

"You got the checks?"

She closed the door. "Yes." She was excited to be leaving, out of breath. "Here."

"Keep them for a minute." The envelopes left his hand. "When's she coming to pick us up?" Another waitress with a car was to drive them into the city.

"In about ten minutes. You all packed?"

He nodded. Ten minutes would not be enough time to say all he wanted to her, but it would have to do. "Come here and sit down." He was surprised how hard his voice sounded.

The bed lowered as she sat. There was not enough time to build up to it although he wanted to be kind. "Look, I ain't going to New York."

She replied quickly. "Where're we going?" She did not understand.

He shook his head. "We ain't going nowhere. But you going to New York."

He listened hard for her reaction, but picked up nothing. Finally: "Where're you going then?"

"I don't know yet. I just know I ain't going to New York, not now anyway. Maybe someday. I don't think I want to live like them people, but I ain't sure."

"Well, neither do I want to live that way." She spoke flatly, just the slightest edge of fear and pain to her words. "Why can't I go with you, Ludlow?"

"Why you want to go with me?"

"You know why." The question must have seemed a silly one. "I love you."

234

"That ain't good enough." He paused. "You know why I ain't going back to New York now?"

"You said," she started nervously, "you said you didn't want to live like people live in New York."

"Like what?"

"You didn't want to take their money."

"What you think of that?" He had to show her why she could not go with him.

"But you can, Ludlow. You can live any way you want. The money wouldn't make any difference." She was more frightened now.

"It ain't that simple." He shrugged. "Anyway, maybe I'll decide to live like that, but I ain't sure, so I ain't going back now."

"But I can wait with you until you decide."

He reached out and put his hand on her knee. "You think I should go back there, don't you? You think it's my big chance."

She spoke into her lap. "Yes."

"I ain't saying you wrong. I'm just saying I don't know if you right. I don't know if it worth my time to go back there and play for them people. I might want to play in one of them little store-front churches where I know folks'll be listening. I don't know yet. But you ain't got the same feelings and there's no reason for you to go with me. You think New York's just fine."

"I don't care what you think I think." She had become angry even while he talked. "I'm going with you. I love you."

She would follow him from city to city, from hotel to hotel if he did not stop her now. "I know you love me, Harriet. And I know something else too. I just realized it. I love you." It was a lie, but as he spoke, he felt suddenly warm and naked at the same time. He kissed her quickly so she would not see his face until he knew it was under his control.

She sighed. "Really, Ludlow?"

He nodded. "Really."

"Finally." He thought she might be crying, placed his fingers on the ledge of bone beneath her eye, but found it dry.

He went on: "If I didn't love you, I'd let you come with me. What the hell! You your own boss. But now, loving you, I wouldn't be happy with you tagging along, especially if I knew you didn't think I was right. I don't want to worry about that."

"But you don't have to worry about me." She was defiant. "I'll take care of myself, Ludlow."

"Maybe I don't got to worry about you, but I would, now wouldn't I?"

She did not answer him. "But you may come to New York?"

"Sure, I may come back." He lied again. "In fact, I think I'm coming back for sure, but I need some more time to think it over."

"If you came, how would I know?"

"Hell, you'd know. But I tell you what—you leave your address with Hardie. Okay?"

She did not like it, was still suspicious, but she agreed.

They sat silently for a few minutes. It began to rain while they waited, the drops at first no closer together than heartbeats, gradually increasing to one loud drone. Then tires were swirled through the mud and water outside and a horn sounded. Harriet got up and went to the window. "That's her. You sure—"

He nodded, stopping her question. She took her suitcase off the bed, kissed his cheek and, wordlessly, went out onto the rain-thumping porch, suddenly cut off by the closing door.

He followed the car in a two-part turn and out the gate, until it disappeared behind the droning above him. Then, slowly, he fell back until his head touched the papered wall behind him. He wondered if it was raining in New York too, or even in New

Marsails. Perhaps he might even go to New Marsails and visit Etta-Sue; he could do that now. Or he could try to find Ragan. He smiled; neither of them would want him to visit, and he did not particularly want to call on either of them. There were other, better places to go. He might find that store-front church, or perhaps a church on a dirt road in the South, no more than a shack, with a congregation of twelve or so, without an organ to help their high, shaky voices carry the tunes of their hymns. A place like that would need a good musician.

About the Author

William Melvin Kelley was born November 1, 1937 in New York City, and attended Harvard University. In addition to *A Drop of Patience*, he is the author of *A Different Drummer, dem, Dancers on the Shore*, and *Dunfords Travels Everywheres*. He currently teaches at Sarah Lawrence College.